14.95

F   NAIPAUL

LOVE AND DEATH IN A
HOT COUNTRY

		DATE DUE	

LOVE AND DEATH IN A HOT COUNTRY

SHIVA NAIPAUL

LOVE AND DEATH

IN A

HOT COUNTRY

The Viking Press
New York

For Savi, who taught me,
and Melo

Published in 1984 by The Viking Press
40 West 23rd Street, New York, N.Y. 10010

Originally published in Great Britain under the title *A Hot Country*.

Library of Congress Cataloging in Publication Data
Naipaul, Shiva, 1945–
  Love and death in a hot country.
  I. Title.
PR9272.9.N3L6   1984   813   83-40245
ISBN 0-670-44211-9

Printed in the United States of America
Set in Times Roman

In this country she was afraid. But it was her soul more than her body that knew fear. She had thought that each individual had a complete self, a complete soul, an accomplished I. And now she realised . . . that this was not so.

D. H. LAWRENCE
The Plumed Serpent

Chapter One

Sometimes – once or twice a year – the Amerindians would come into Charlestown.

How blank they were. How silent. She had gazed fascinated at those broad, flat faces which told of nothing. They would squat on the pavements around the market. A father, a mother, a baby. Around themselves they spread their wares: blankets, baskets, trinkets. Occasionally there were birds of beautiful plumage caught in the deep forest. She used to be a little afraid of them.

They were a reminder of the vastness of Cuyama; of the wilderness that lay behind their backs.

The jungle at their backs – and, facing them, the Atlantic, rolling its brown waves: a tepid, sullen sea laden with the silt of a continent's great rivers.

Cuyama, a tract of land perched uneasily on the sloping shoulder of South America, a degree or two north of the Equator. Cuyama, a tract of land on the fringe of an Empire whose interests had always lain elsewhere.

On their blue copybooks were portraits of British kings and queens.

It was told how Sir Walter Raleigh had come to this wilderness. But he had found nothing worth finding – only the overwhelming forest and tribes of miserable aboriginals; men barely progressed beyond the Stone Age; who painted their bodies; who lived off roots and small wild animals; who shot fish with poisoned arrows; who, occasionally, hunted each other's heads. He came and went away to be beheaded in the Tower of London.

1

Sitting on the windy veranda of the school-house, she grew sleepy in the afternoon heat. Dust rose in swirls from the stony playground, powdering the feathery leaves of the tamarind tree that grew there. How old was she? Probably nine or ten. A meagre, brown-skinned girl with plaited hair tied with red ribbons.

Far away, on the spacious plains of Central Asia (so she learned from another of her books), the Kirghiz were living in tents of hide. In the spring, when the snows had begun to melt, they would take their flocks up to the high pastures where the spring flowers would be coming into bloom.

Snow.

Spring flowers.

Rich pastures.

A pinch on the arm restored her to attention.

– What is the population of Cuyama?

– Just over one million.

– Where do the vast majority of the Cuyamese people live?

– On the coastal plains.

– What is the main cash crop of Cuyama?

– Sugar-cane.

She watched the clouds of golden dust swirling up from the playground, settling on the leaves of the tamarind tree.

The jungle at their backs ... and, in between it and the brown ocean – the endless, waving fields of sugar-cane.

– After the Spaniards, which nation ruled Cuyama?

– The Dutch.

– That is so. For nearly one hundred years the Dutch ruled Cuyama. Their legacy persists in the names of many of our towns and villages. Can you name any of these towns and villages?

– New Utrecht.

– Alkmaar.

– Groningen.

Teacher hitched up the sleeves of his cream-coloured shirt, stained with circles of sweat at the arm-pits.

2

– It was the Dutch who first drained the coastal swamps of our country and who first built dykes to protect us from the high tides of the Atlantic. It was a task for which they were particularly well suited because their own country was very low-lying and flat, some of it below sea-level. On the reclaimed lands and along the banks of the rivers, they established their plantations. The remains of some of those early plantations can still be seen. In those days they did not only grow sugar-cane. Cotton, tobacco and indigo were also cultivated. But what did the establishment of these plantations mean? Can anyone tell me?

– Slavery.

– Correct. It meant the enslavement of thousands of human beings. To work the land, thousands of Africans were taken away from their country, brought across the ocean packed like cattle in the holds of sailing ships. They were transported like cattle and sold like cattle to the highest bidder. For us that is almost impossible to imagine. Yet it happened. It happened right here in Charlestown.

She stared at Teacher, at his smooth, black face, moistened with sweat. He could not have been much more than twenty years old, if that. Every morning she would watch him wheel his bicycle into the playground, carefully chain it to the fence, bend down and remove his bicycle clips and delicately shake straight his creased trousers. Early in the day, he smelled of eau de cologne. By noon, however, its freshness would have evaporated from his skin.

– Cuyama became rich. Vast fortunes were made here. The planters built themselves Great Houses, mansions with pillared porches. You can also see the ruins of those along the river banks. Some ate off plates made from gold.

The smooth, black face was transformed into a mysterious mask. Those plates of gold! The class was awestruck.

– Yet, despite the wealth they laboured in the fields to create, the slaves were harshly treated. Babies would be drowned because their crying disturbed the master or mis-

3

tress. Slaves who displeased their master were mercilessly whipped. They would be tortured, branded with red-hot irons, buried alive, mutilated. Cuyama became notorious for its cruelty. The African was not regarded as human and the land ran with blood.

Teacher mopped his face with a handkerchief. The sweat stains expanded across the back of his shirt.

She dreamt of the Kirghiz leading their flocks up to the spring pastures dappled with the loveliest of wild flowers.

In the playground, the dust-devils took shape and died away.

– Time and again the slaves rose in rebellion. They ran off from the plantations and disappeared into the woods where the white man was afraid to follow them. Leaders arose among them and armies were created. The struggle between master and slave was ceaseless. Eventually, the white men offered peace to the escaped slaves. They said, 'We will not interfere with you if you promise not to interfere with us. You may live as you wish in the woods.' And so, gradually, peace was made. Today the descendants of those runaway slaves still live in the woods, following their own ways and their own customs. What do we call them?

– Bush Folk.

– That is right. We call them the Bush Folk. The Dutch were greatly weakened by these wars with their slaves. Many of the planters left for other places and their estates fell into decay. Finally the Dutch were expelled. Who took their place?

– The French.

– Yes, the French took their place. But their rule did not last long. They were soon replaced by the British. Why should we Cuyamese be grateful to the British?

– They abolished slavery.

– And who was the Englishman responsible for that?

– William Wilberforce.

Teacher smiled at them, beating a ruler against his palms.

– It was only natural that the emancipated slaves should not want to stay on the plantations. Those places held too many bad memories for them. So they went away from those places of bad memory. It was because of this that the British brought in labour from other countries. Hindustanis were brought over from India, Chinese from China, Javanese from the island of Java. Even Portuguese were brought out to Cuyama. So it was that all the people we call Cuyamese came together, creating a blend of many peoples, many religions, many cultures. All different and still all Cuyamese.

They looked at him and at each other and did not know what to think or how to respond.

There they were: a million people trapped in the sun-stunned vacuum separating ocean from jungle.

*

Tears ... out of their stale, salt taste was distilled an image of herself sprawled on the bare floorboards. Outside it was almost dark. Grace was practising her scales on the piano. The sounds, drifting past her, vanished through the open windows of the room, mingling with the oncoming darkness. Her throat was parched. Her mind ballooned with vacancy. She lay there in perfect stillness, listening to Grace, staring at the curving spine of a coconut tree growing in one of the neighbouring yards, tasting on her dessicated lips the salt of dried tears.

The previous evening she had told Grace she did not believe in God.

'When we Cuyamese die,' she had said to her, 'we don't go to either Heaven or Hell. There's no Heaven and no Hell for us to go to. Our skin and bones will rot in our graves. There'll be nothing left of us. Not a trace.'

Even now she did not fully understand what had prompted that outburst. Maybe it was because she had been watching Grace prinking and preening in front of the mirror,

5

contemplating with complacent salaciousness the outlines of her budding breasts visible beneath the transparency of her nightdress.

Grace had stared at her with dilated eyes.

'You don't know what you saying,' she said.

She laughed, disguising the alarm she had begun to feel.

'I going to tell Papa,' Grace said.

'Tell whoever you like.' She turned away from her.

Her spasm of elation vanished as swiftly as it had arisen. It was not only the fear of what her father would do which unnerved her. Something else, a vague sense of foreboding for which she had no name, had clamped itself on her heart. The temptation to retract was strong. She would have liked to say to Grace, 'Don't tell on me. Don't tell Papa. I didn't really mean those things I just said.'

Yet, she did nothing of the kind. She lay on the bed beside her sister, staring at the glowing mosquito coil burning on the floor at the foot of the bed, savouring her terror.

Nothing had happened, however, until her return from school the following day. As they sat around the table having their afternoon tea – one of the family's rituals – she wondered if Grace had forgotten or decided not to tell. Grace's face gave nothing away. Nor did her father's. She watched and waited, forcing herself to eat. At that moment she did not know which was the greater: disappointment that, after all, nothing might happen to her; or relief at the possibility of an unexpected reprieve. It was only when her mother had started to clear the table that her father glanced in her direction. 'Come and see me in the school-room,' he said.

The 'school-room' was an annexe tacked on to the rear of the house. In it her father continued his schoolmasterly labours in after-hours, providing extra tuition for the boys he taught by day – and for anyone else who cared to pay for the privilege of having their sons taught by him. He had acquired a reputation for being able to whip the best out of the most unpromising material. It was a dismal place furnished with rough wooden benches and trestle tables, a blackboard and a desk. One rarely ventured voluntarily into that penitential domain.

Greying head drooping towards his chest, he sat at the desk which was cluttered, as always, with copybooks, coloured pencils and broken sticks of chalk. She stared at the bony, chalk-stained fingers sprouting greying hairs and the wrists ridged with upstanding veins running blue-grey beneath the taut skin. They told of a life-time of unremitting labour; of rigorous effort narrowly directed towards the narrowest of ends. Behind him was the curtainless window, framing the arching trunk of the coconut tree and the corrugated-iron roofs of the neighbouring houses. Arithmetical calculations were scrawled across the blackboard. She stood before the desk, hands hanging limp against the pleated skirt of her school uniform, gazing out at the view, listening to the shouts and shrieks of the children playing in the yard next door. At last he raised his head and looked at her. His glasses, reflecting the bleak contours of the room, hid his eyes from her.

'Did you tell Grace that you did not believe in God?' His voice was level and controlled, but the muscles at the corner of his mouth twitched.

Her throat had gone dry.

'Answer me.'

'Papa ...'

'Answer me.'

'I didn't mean it, Papa.'

'If you didn't mean it, why did you say it?'

'I don't know, Papa.'

'You didn't mean it and you don't know why you said it.' He picked up one of the broken sticks of chalk and rolled it between his fingers. 'Do you know what blasphemy is?'

'Yes, Papa.'

'Are you aware of what happens to blasphemers?'

7

She breathed with difficulty.

'Answer me.'

'Yes, Papa.'

He got up and, turning his back on her, gazed out at the fading afternoon. 'I've built my life on faith in Christ,' he said. 'If there was no God there would be no reason for anything. Life would be one big joke.' He swung round to face her. 'Is my life a joke to you?'

She stared at him dumbly.

He pulled open one of the drawers of the desk. Taking from it a stout leather strap, he came towards her. She raised her hands and covered her face.

'Kneel.'

She knelt before him. He stood over her.

'Say after me: Our Father Which Art In Heaven . . .'

'Our Father Which Art In Heaven . . .'

She saw the strap descending a steep arc. Her shoulders ignited.

'Hallowed Be Thy Name . . .'

'Hallowed Be Thy Name . . .'

Again the strap descended.

'Thy Kingdom Come, Thy Will Be Done . . .'

'Thy Kingdom Come, Thy Will Be Done . . .'

Her whole body seemed to burst into flame. Barely conscious of what she was doing, screams rising out of her throat, she lunged at his legs, struggling with him for possession of the strap, biting and scratching and kicking at him. But he was too strong for her.

'On Earth As It Is In Heaven . . .'

'On Earth As It Is In Heaven . . .'

She must have fainted, for when next she became aware of herself darkness had fallen and Grace was practising her scales. For an hour or more, she remained sprawled open-eyed and motionless on the floorboards. In the early hours of the morning she came to again. At first, she was confused. Then she saw the glow of the mosquito coil burning on the floor at the foot of the bed. Her father must have come for her at some point in the night. He must have taken her up in his arms and brought her to bed. It may have been he who rubbed some soothing ointment into the welts disfiguring her back and shoulders.

No open reference was made to the incident after that, though for nearly a week she ran a fever and stayed away from school. On his return from work in the afternoons, he would go to her room. They did not speak much. Once, his fingers tender and caressing, he examined her injuries.

'Does it still hurt?' he asked.

She shook her head.

He seemed to want to say something else. But, whatever it was, it remained unsaid.

He had never again beaten her. He seemed – but this may have been her imagination – to lose some of his energy; to become tireder and older. 'Is my life a joke?' he had asked. It must suddenly have dawned on him that it was. The horror of that revelation pained her now, not the bruises he had inflicted on her in his frenzy. On certain evenings, sunk into himself, he would sit out on the rocking-chair on the little fern-embowered veranda, gazing out at the street and the dreary houses. She could still hear the slow creaking of that rocking-chair.

Once, he had called her out to him. He had taken her on his lap. For a while they rocked together in awkward silence.

'*Mallingham*,' he muttered suddenly, '*Mallingham*.' He gazed wryly into her face and smiled.

She had failed to understand at the time.

They had been bred on his narrow certainties. Their lives rarely strayed from the path he had marked out for them: a path summed up by the ever-recurring phrase, 'Remember, we are a *Christian* family.'

Above their front door was a framed depiction of Christ on the Cross.

A Christian family.

9

Chapter Two

Dina, eyes shielded by dark glasses, sat on the bench looking at the child. Clara was bending forward, peering at something that lay on the grass.

'What is it?' she called out. 'What are you looking at?' The child did not answer.

'What is it?' she called out again – more irritably.

Still the child offered no reply. Reluctantly, stifling her irritation, she walked over to where Clara stood. There, lying on the grass, was a tiny yellow and black bird. Where once its eyes had been, there were holes. Its wings were almost torn away from its frail body. It lay there, shrivelled and lustreless; hopelessly dead.

'Go away,' she said. 'Leave it alone.'

Clara seemed not to hear. She nudged the corpse with the tip of her dusty shoe.

'I told you to leave it alone. It's dead.'

Clara glanced up at her. Slowly, she straightened herself. Slowly, she walked away.

Dina stared at the eyeless, broken-winged creature. Birds like this one came every day to their little garden. They came in the early morning and late afternoon, fluttering among the blossoms of the bleeding-heart vine that grew over the back fence, their plumage flashing in the sunlight, hiding from the heat of noonday among the dark leaves of the orange tree. It had never occurred to her that their ends could be so violent, so terrible. This merciless rending of feather and flesh and bone was so out of proportion to the scale of their existence. Turning away, she went back to her bench.

She sat there, one pale, brown arm extended along the back of the bench, her skin sheened with the moist afternoon heat. These excursions with Clara had only recently become part of her daily routine: a belated show of maternal responsibility. Aubrey was pleased, although he scrupulously avoided saying anything that might suggest she had been guilty of neglect. The sadness was that these excursions had not brought her any closer to the child. They had remained strangers to each other, awkward and clumsy in their rare attempts at affection. She was playing at being a mother; Clara was playing at being her child. Afternoon upon afternoon she sat on that bench, looking up at the hills patterned with shifting cloud-shadows, watching Clara play her solitary games, longing for the moment of release when, once more, she could surrender her to her father and Selma.

Behind her were the gloomy glades of the Botanical Gardens. To her left, behind a high hedge, rose the grey, balconied façade of the Presidential Mansion – formerly the residence of the territory's British governors. From a tall pole flapped the green, red and yellow flag, symbol of the nation's Independence. Beyond rose the blue hills. Clara had climbed into the circular bandstand in the centre of the garden. For years no music had come from it. With its green-painted conical roof and fretted eaves it had acquired the look of a modestly-conceived folly. Not far from the bandstand, by the wrought-iron gates giving access to the Presidential Mansion, a pair of helmeted soldiers stood erect. They held bayonetted rifles. Apart from herself, Clara and the soldiers, there was no one else to be seen. She could hear but not see the traffic on the busy road separating this little oasis from Independence Park.

The light was becoming yellower. Shadows were growing long across the grass. The bougainvillaea glowed red and purple. It was time for them to be going. She signalled to Clara who came obediently forward.

11

'I'll buy you a coconut on the way home,' she said. 'Would you like that?'

Clara assented mutely to the offer.

She turned away, walking towards the gloom of the Botanical Gardens. Together but separate, mother and daughter moved along the network of asphalted paths winding under trees burdened with vines, ferns and parasites of all kinds. Elephantine limbs, greened with moss, spread and arched high above their heads. From each trailed twisted ropes of lianas. Browning leaves littered the vistas of grass. Now and then a tremor of warm air agitated the scattered groves of palms and bamboo, stirring up rich, steamy odours of vegetable decay, of jungly profusion: a gentle reminder that theirs was a land three-quarters of whose surface was covered with virginal forest.

There was no one else about – there seldom was. Now and then Dina might come across a man lazily scything the grass or catch a glimpse of a body sprawled in the shade of a tree. Occasionally, she might disturb a pair of strolling lovers. On most of her visits, however, she had the place to herself. The meandering paths along which they walked were gradually crumbling away, cratered with holes which were only rarely repaired. Weeds sprouted in the fissures that had opened up in the asphalt. Dina trod warily beneath the labyrinthine limbs coiling overhead, staring at the names painted on to boards nailed to the boles.

Coroupita Guianensis.

Bertholletia Excelsa.

Caryocar Butyrosum.

A dead language in a dying place. Some of the boards had rotted away and not been replaced. Others had weathered into indecipherability. Clara, as she often did, paused by the banyan, wandering off among its dusty columns. Nearby was the main road, ringing the desert expanse of Independence Park. A flock of parrots squawked into the leafy dusk of the Gardens.

'We must go,' she said to Clara. 'It will be dark soon.'
In Charlestown it was not safe to be out after dark.

They crossed the road, negotiated the collapsed iron railings that had once fenced off the park and resumed their homeward journey. On the far side rose the cream-coloured, curving façade of the Park Hotel. To the west she could see the rippling plain of the Gulf, blooded with the colours of sunset. A bank of cloud, its billowing heart tinged with orange and purple, was stretched across the horizon. Closer to the shore, ships rode at anchor. But, the park descending, they soon lost sight of the ships and the sea. Groups of ragged boys played games of football on improvised pitches scattered about the waste. A galloping horse raised a fog of dust on the exercise track. They emerged opposite the Park Hotel. Here there were many more people. Food stalls and coconut carts lined the roadside.

She glanced at Clara. 'Well?'

'Yes,' Clara replied.

She approached the nearest coconut cart, tended by a wild-looking Hindustani man dressed in a frayed khaki shirt and short, equally frayed khaki trousers. He chopped and sliced with his cutlass and handed the coconut to Clara.

'Be careful,' Dina said. 'If the water drips on your dress the stain will never come off.'

Clara drank gingerly, chin tilted upwards.

Say No To The Exploiter! Vote Yes!

The slogan, executed in blood-red lettering, was daubed across the width of the pavement. Posters bearing the official effigy of the President – lava-smooth face, sleepy eyes, stiff-collared tunic buttoned up to the neck – encrusted the lamp-posts. A banner was suspended over the entrance to the forecourt of the Park Hotel. 'Black Men,' it proclaimed, 'Have Nothing To Lose But Their Chains.' A liveried flunkey stood by the glass doors which were approached up a flight of steps lined with potted palms. Subdued lights illuminated the lobby behind him. As she watched, the flunkey, with a flourish, threw open the glass doors. A white man wearing a bush shirt and carrying a briefcase appeared.

'Honky!'

The flunkey blew a whistle. A taxi crept to the foot of the steps.

'White trash!'

She saw herself in a bridal dress coming down those palm-lined steps. Aubrey, a white carnation adorning the lapel of his jacket, was holding her arm. Grains of rice were falling on her head, pattering in a fine rain on the stone steps: an event as unreal now as it had been then.

Clara tossed the shell of the coconut into the back of the cart.

'Was that good?' Dina asked, drying the child's fingers and chin with her handkerchief.

Clara nodded.

Crossing the road, they continued homeward. Clara ran on ahead when they turned the corner of the street. The blackened wall of the Anglican Church threw its shadow across the street. Its lower reaches were daubed with streaks of red and white paint, disfigured with posters.

Kill The Nigger In You.

One Nation. One Party. One Redeemer.

And it was there, in the shadow cast by the church, not twenty yards from the door of the bookshop, she saw it. Its black face was mockingly turned up towards her, washed up to a standstill against the mossy curb. She started, stopped, stared at it. It was not an hallucination. There, plainly and undeniably, it lay: discoloured, dog-eared and frayed, surrounded by a sodden drift of leaves, bits of wood and glass and a crushed cigarette packet.

She bent down, reaching for it. Then, recollecting herself, she straightened up and looked round to see if there had been any witnesses to her strange behaviour. A man was loping towards her from the far end of the street. But it was unlikely that he would have noticed anything. The nearby

14

verandas were untenanted. What would the neighbours have thought if they had seen her, the wife of Aubrey St Pierre, reaching into the gutter, retrieving from the sewage with her bare hands a filthy, crumpled playing card? Or, come to that, what would Aubrey have thought?

She turned away, looking towards the park and the line of darkening hills beyond the turrets of the Presidential Mansion. The lower slopes were scarred with quarrying. If the wind was blowing in the right direction, you could sometimes hear the muffled explosions. It must have been blowing in the right direction that afternoon for, as she lingered in the shade of the church, the boom of a detonation reached her. 'I will lift up mine eyes unto the hills, whence cometh my help . . .' The lines of the psalm she had so often sung as a child rolled up unbidden. 'I will lift up mine eyes, and there will be no hills, no help . . .' She smiled.

Aubrey had come out to the gateway of the bookshop in search of her. Clara was perched on his shoulders.

'Have you lost something?' He eased the child to the ground, looking intently into her face with the round, dark eyes he had passed on to his daughter. A blue smock flowed with voluminous elegance from a pair of narrow, sloping shoulders. His sandalled feet were sockless.

'No. I haven't lost anything. I was just . . .' She shrugged, shying away from his solicitude. 'I was just looking at the hills. That's all. What do they do with all the rock they keep taking from there?' The black face of the card danced before her.

'They're building roads in the Interior. "Opening up the Interior," they call it.' He smiled ironically, playing with the fringe of his sparse beard. 'The rock's transported up-river by barge.'

'What about the mountains in the Interior? Why don't they quarry those?'

He smiled again. 'They're far too remote.'

'Tell about the dead bird.' Clara tugged at her skirt.

15

'What dead bird?' Aubrey tousled the child's hair.

'We saw a dead bird in the garden. One of those tiny yellow and black ones.'

'How sad,' Aubrey said.

'It had no eyes,' Clara said.

Aubrey patted Clara's head. 'Don't think about it.'

The twilight was thickening rapidly. She glanced towards the spot where she had seen the card lying in the gutter. They went into the bookshop, a cube of fluorescent glitter in the dusk. Aubrey sat down at his leather-topped desk, strewn with books and papers, where he had been going through invoices. Clara clung to his knees.

She watched them. Father and Daughter.

'I'll make some tea,' she said.

'Why don't you let Selma do that? You look quite worn out.' The look of solicitude reasserted itself.

'I'm fine.' She went through the curtained doorway that led to the house proper. In the tiny kitchen, away from Aubrey and Clara, she struggled to steady herself with the soothing ritual.

*

Carrying the tea on a tray, she returned to the bookshop. Clara had disappeared, gone off, no doubt, in search of Selma. Aubrey was hunched over his desk, frowning at the invoices. She rested the tray on the desk.

'I'm beginning to wonder how much longer I can keep this up.' He sighed.

'Did you sell anything today?'

'A paperback!' He laughed, throwing down the pen he was holding, cradling his head in his palms.

She looked at the bent head with its thinning hair. It was not often he allowed himself the luxury of complaint.

'And yet, if I were to admit defeat and close down, what would we do then?' He stared up at her. 'Emigrate like all the

16

rest? Go and find ourselves some snow-bound Canadian haven?'

She poured the tea. The fluorescent tubes on the ceiling flickered and crackled.

'I'm sorry,' he murmured after a pause. 'I shouldn't be burdening you with this nonsense. I'm a little tired. It must be this awful weather we've been having.' He smiled. 'How was your day?'

'Much as usual.'

'Clara enjoys her walks with you.' He spoke hesitantly. 'I think they've done her a lot of good.'

She drank her tea. It was obvious that there was more he would have liked to say. An awkward silence intervened. Overhead, the fluorescent tubes flickered and crackled. The dark street was quiet.

She dwelt on the image of the card she had seen in the gutter. 'Are you superstitious?' she asked suddenly.

Delicately, he replaced his cup on its saucer. He considered her. 'Why do you ask?'

'I just wondered.'

'It depends on what you mean by the word,' he said. 'Some so-called superstitions have been shown to have some basis to them. I keep an open mind. What kind of superstitions are you referring to?'

'Do you believe that there are such things as signs, as omens . . . stuff like that?' She was beginning to regret her indiscretion.

Aubrey smiled, playing with the fringe of his beard. 'No,' he said. 'Stuff like that I don't believe in. I'm a rationalist. Surely you know that.' He raised his eyebrows at her.

'Of course. You're a rationalist. I was forgetting.'

Indistinct figures prowled along the dark street. She blinked into the constantly altering fluorescent glare. The electric storm on the ceiling began to rage with greater ferocity: the room went black.

Aubrey groaned. She listened to him stumbling and groping about the room. A match scraped and flared. Candles bloomed into flame. The bookshop, transformed by the soft, shifting patterns of light and shadow, lost its strident solidity. It became a wavering, dissolving cave, grotesquely mutable, possessed of a life all its own. Going back to the desk, Aubrey once more cradled his head in his palms.

'How long do you suppose it will last this time?' she asked.

'Who knows?' He fluttered his hands resignedly. 'Now there's even talk about a shortage of candles.'

'Is there?' Her tone was idly conversational. She stared out at the black street.

'So it's rumoured. If it's true, it means that the age of darkness will soon be literally upon us. We shall have to develop the eyes of bats. Or, rather, their radar equipment.' He laughed.

'Beatrice has been hoarding candles for months.'

Aubrey's face soured into severity. 'That's not the solution. It's part of the problem. Beatrice should know better.'

She said nothing.

'What prompted your question just now?'

'What question?'

'About being superstitious. Signs and omens.' He scanned her face. 'Was it that dead bird you and Clara saw?'

'It's not important.' She rose, gathering up the tea things, stacking them on the tray.

'Do tell me.'

'I saw a card in the gutter not far from here. It's quite stupid. Not worth talking about.'

'What kind of card?' The guttering flame of the candle on his desk was reflected in his pupils.

It was to those twin lances of yellow light to which she now addressed herself. 'An ordinary playing card. The six of spades.'

'Why should that disturb you?'

'It's a card I keep seeing. Or believe I keep seeing.'

'I don't understand.'

'There's nothing much to understand.' She stared at those twin yellow lances.

'And so that was why you were looking as if you had seen a ghost.' He spoke to himself rather than to her, his forehead furrowing.

A rippling draught set the candle flames dancing. The unstable, cave-like atmosphere quivered and dissolved. In that chaos of leaping light and shadow she felt giddy. To steady herself, she clutched at the edge of the desk. Aubrey, fortunately, did not notice.

'There could be a dozen different reasons for that card being where it was.' He shook his head at her. 'You shouldn't allow yourself to be troubled by such foolishness. Also, you most probably delude yourself when you think you see it more often than any other card. You've simply trained yourself to notice that particular card.'

The room had settled down again; been restored to a semblance of order and solidity.

'I'm sure you're perfectly correct.' She picked up the tray.

He got up. 'Dina . . . it's all nonsense. Neurotic nonsense. You're too intelligent not to be aware of that.' He rested a hand on her shoulder. 'Once you predispose yourself to that kind of belief almost anything can be interpreted in accordance with it. You can see signs and omens in the shape of a cloud, the flight of a flock of birds, the markings on a shell.' The sleeves of his smock billowed as he swept his arms upward. 'And what do you suppose your card portends? What do you think it's trying to tell you?'

'I don't know.'

She moved towards the curtained doorway. Fizzing, crackling, the fluorescent tubes smouldered and sparked into uncertain life. She stopped, dazzled, and looked back at him from the doorway; she laughed. 'The age of darkness is not yet upon us. Rationality – light – has prevailed.'

'It has to prevail. Otherwise we're all lost.' He watched her sombrely.

19

'We were all lost a long time ago, don't you think? You
... me ... everybody ever born in this god-forsaken hole.'
'No. I don't believe that. Nor should you.'
She laughed again and went through to the kitchen.
After she had gone, Aubrey paced about the little shop,
his arms folded across his chest. Deciding there would be no
more business that day, he began closing up the shop.

*

She had laughed at him and at herself. But that evening,
lying in bed in the thick, overheated darkness, the fear had
returned and this time, as if trapped by the night's silence,
she was not able to get rid of it so easily. It came upon her in
waves, tightening her belly, racing her heart. Again and
again she saw the sodden heap of leaves, the slivers of wood,
the shining splinters of glass, the crushed cigarette packet.
How had it got there? What chain of events had led that card
to come to rest virtually on her doorstep? And what, at that
particular moment, had made her look down into the gutter?
It was not her habit to let her eyes sweep along the gutters as
she walked. Normally, she carried herself erect, head tilted
slightly back, her face angled towards the sky. What had
prompted her to look down at precisely that moment? If she
had done so two paces before or two paces after, she would
not have seen it.

Her heart thumped with disconcerting loudness against
the pillow. To banish the sound, she drew herself up, leaning
against the headboard, listening to the ticking of the bedside
alarm. She looked down at Aubrey, breathing evenly and
reposefully. At length, she got out of bed altogether, went to
the window, opened the curtains and looked down at the
street. An electrically illuminated cross crowned the roof of
the church, lighting up the night with a blue glow which
glimmered palely on the leaves of the trees growing in the
church yard. A beacon flashed red on the ridge of the hills
whose mutilated escarpments had disappeared into the

moonless night. The street was a shadowy river of tranquillity. Was it, she wondered, still lying there, wreathed by the gutter's wrack? She peered towards the spot – as if, miraculously, out of those impenetrable shadows, an answer would be given her.

*

It was on her honeymoon she had last sat like this at a window, gripped by a similar panic, a similar dread. The train from Venice had brought them across the plains of northern Italy to a small lakeside town. A taxi had taken them up to a small hotel on a wooded hill overlooking the town. It was not the tourist season and they were the hotel's only guests. Their schedule had been hectic – during the space of three weeks it had taken them first to England and then, travelling by trains, across half of Western Europe. On that first night in the lakeside town, after a day of rain and drifting mist, the sky had cleared to reveal a full moon. Unable to fall asleep, she had drawn a chair up to the window and gazed out upon the Alps and the moonlit lake far below. 'Nearly two thousand years ago,' Aubrey had said as they lingered over their bottle of wine after dinner, 'Hannibal brought his elephants and his Carthaginian army over those mountains to conquer mighty Rome. Can you imagine it?' 'No,' she had replied. She remembered how peculiarly he had looked at her. Their grand tour had brought to the fore Aubrey's pedagogical instinct.

Everything had happened so swiftly – Aubrey's unexpected proposal, her own equally unexpected acceptance, the swift ceremony in the Registry Office – her chief memory of that was the funereal odour of Beatrice's perfume swirling through the small room – the noisy, overcrowded reception in the ballroom of the Park Hotel, the grains of rice falling on her head and pattering on the stone steps, the journey out to the airport, the long flight to London . . . each event had followed the other in such swift succession that she had

had no opportunity to reflect on what was happening to her. Still, that was how she had wanted it to be: to be carried along by the sheer momentum of events. The swiftness, the turmoil, had acted like an anaesthetic on her.

But that night, sitting at the window, staring at the moon-lit water, with Aubrey breathing evenly behind her, the numbness had begun to wear off and the naked realisation of what she had done had suddenly come upon her out of the shadows. The man with whom she shared this room under the Alps was her 'husband'. She, whom the world now called Dina St Pierre, was his 'wife'. *Her* husband! *His* wife! There had to be some mistake somewhere. She had to be dream-ing. But sitting there at that window, staring at the shining lake, listening to Aubrey's measured inhalations and exhala-tions, she knew it was no dream. She knew it was no dream and yet she was overwhelmed by incredulity. She had turned away from the window to look at the stranger's body stretched out on the white sheets – those starched, pallid sheets striped blue by the moon whose radiance sluiced through the shutters. How long had she sat at that window staring at him? It seemed as if she had looked at him for hours; as though desperately hoping that the intensity of her gaze, of her incredulity, would somehow cause the wraith to vanish and that she would find herself once more alone, far from that moonlit room, far from that turbulence of snowy peaks, far from the phantasmagorial lake glistening below her.

But nothing of the kind had occurred. Instead, Aubrey, becoming aware of her absence, perhaps disturbed by the moonlight bathing his face, had stirred into wakefulness. 'What are you doing?' he asked. 'Why aren't you in bed?' 'I'm admiring the moon on the water,' she said. He had joined her at the window. Together they had looked out in silence at the lake and at those mountains through whose high passes, two thousand years before, Hannibal the Car-thaginian had irrupted with his elephants.

Nearly five years separated that Alpine night from this tropical one. She had never truly recovered from her initial explosion of incredulity. It had, of course, been dulled by the passage of time; been overlaid by habit and routine. But it had never completely disappeared. Every so often, amid the most ordinary of circumstances – talking to him over breakfast, walking along beside him, sitting quietly by herself thinking of nothing in particular, lying sleepless next to him – it would suddenly resurface with all its original force. She would gaze wonderingly at the man who so calmly claimed her as his own, whom the registrar had so calmly consecrated 'husband'. The same sensation had gripped her when the midwife had held up for her dazed inspection a bloodstained creature and announced her motherhood.

*

A faint wash of white showed in the eastern sky. Out of the retreating night there condensed the silhouettes of palm trees, of roof-tops, of the hills. A sullen pink glow appeared on the rim of the horizon. She watched it deepen and spread. Pale gold flushed along the edges of the clouds. Only in the churchyard, among the trees and bushes, did stray scraps of the night seem to linger, trapped in fraying pockets among branches and leaves. A street sweeper arrived, lazily scraping his broom along the gutter, pushing the wrack before him. Cocks crowed. She came away from the window and got into bed. Still, now that the day had come she was less afraid.

Chapter Three

Aubrey would often return to their very first meeting which, like a film, he would play back to himself; freezing, as it were, certain images and subjecting them to a fascinated scrutiny. It was as if some secret were buried there, some clue to his bewilderment. Over and over he replayed that film, watching her, watching himself. Untouched at the time of its happening by any intimation of sorrow, the film did, in retrospect, innocently contain within itself the seed of all that was to come. Yet, it also allowed him to see her as he saw her then – untainted by the bitter knowledge that was to come to him.

The bookshop during the early days of its existence was sited not on that comparative sedate street near Independence Park but, somewhat bizarrely, in a rundown western suburb of Charlestown. Formerly a doctor's surgery, it occupied a corner site on a busy main road lined with rum-shops, cheap eating-houses, grimy workshops devoted to repairing the irreparable and 'guest houses' of dubious intent. On one side the Aurora (so Aubrey had named his enterprise) was companioned by a popular and noisy rum-shop – the Serenity Bar – where, day and night, a juke-box thumped out its special brand of comfort to a clientele who, frequently, would emerge from its murky interior to relieve themselves on the pavement, or to be sick, or to collapse in sudden stupefaction. Directly opposite was a decaying cinema.

It was not, on the face of it, the ideal location from which to launch a project dedicated to the elevation of the Cuyamese intellect. However, at that juncture, the former surgery was the only suitable premises Aubrey could find at a reasonable rent. Not wishing to delay the setting up of the enterprise, he had, despite all advice to the contrary, gone ahead and installed himself in the unlikely spot. 'It's exactly the sort of place where a bookshop like mine is most desperately needed,' he said.

The film began, as always, with the taxi coming to a halt beyond the sagging wire fence which ineffectually shielded the Aurora from the incursions of the drunks emerging from the Serenity Bar. Sitting at his desk, he had watched the young woman, quietly and respectably dressed, half of her face hidden behind a pair of dark glasses, a handbag of weathered leather looped over one shoulder, step out of the car. Smoothing down her skirt, she had glanced up at the signboard projecting like a stiffened flag from its pole. In bold, black lettering it proclaimed the Aurora's existence – Books To Feed The Mind And Gladden The Soul – announced that browsers were welcome, and stated its hours of business.

She lingered on the pavement, absently smoothing her skirt and reading the sign. With an air of uncertainty, she looked round her, taking in the detail of the immediate neighbourhood, staring at the Serenity Bar and the peeling billboards of the cinema across the road. He watched as, with a sudden spurt of resolution, she pushed open the gate and advanced up the fissured concrete path. Uncertainty reasserting itself, she slowed her pace as she ascended the short flight of steps leading into the shop.

She paused in the doorway. Removing her dark glasses, she blinked into the gloom and raised an angled arm in front of her face – as though shielding herself from some impending blow; warding off some undisclosed threat. It was highly unusual to get customers – or even browsers – at the start of the day's business. He rose from the desk and approached her as she stood indecisively in the doorway.

'Can I be of any assistance to you?' he had asked, struck

25

by her vibrating uncertainty: an uncertainty bordering on apprehension.

A sheen of sweat glistened on her forehead, glueing straying strands of her hair to the skin. Her fussed eyes flickered and blinked at him. 'I'm looking for a Mr St Pierre. For a Mr Aubrey St Pierre.' She spoke with a curt rapidity, performing once more her curious, warding-off gesture.

'I am Aubrey St Pierre.'

She seemed to be unprepared for this bit of news. Her restless eyes skated away from contact, scanning the shelves in an unseeing way. 'I've come about the job. The one you advertised. I saw it in the newspaper a few days ago.'

He examined her with greater interest. She was not at all like the dozen or so applicants who had presented themselves to him. They had tended to come from the lower reaches of the social scale – young girls recently released from a cursory secondary schooling, one or two of whom were barely literate. The young woman facing him was altogether different. It had not entered his head as he watched her push open the gate and come up the path that she was one more applicant for the job he had rashly advertised.

'I suppose it's already gone?' She seemed prepared to turn around and go away that instant.

'No, no,' he answered, recovering himself. 'It hasn't gone. It's still very much there.'

He brought the desk chair and invited her to sit down. She did so, smoothing out her skirt, carefully arranging her knees, gazing out at the main road and the billboards. Next door the juke-box thumped.

This was one of the frames he most often froze and re-examined. If at that moment he had said what it had been on the tip of his tongue to say – that he had decided, on reflection, to do without an assistant and was sorry for the inconvenience he had caused her – it would have ended there. She would have gone away from him to be re-absorbed into the limbo out of which she had come. But he had not. Curiosity had got the better of him.

He paced about the shop, rubbing his hands. 'It's proved a difficult post to fill, more difficult than I imagined it would be.' He paused in front of her. 'I don't believe I know your name,' he said.

'Mallingham,' she replied. 'Dina Mallingham.' She removed the handbag from her shoulder, placing it on her lap. She was calmer now; more self-assured.

'To be frank, Miss Mallingham, you don't look like someone who would be interested in the kind of job I'm offering.'

'What are your applicants supposed to look like?' she asked, smiling at him.

He ignored the irony. 'The job really amounts to little more than keeping an eye on things when I'm not around or otherwise occupied. The shop isn't very busy.'

She remained silent.

'Nor is the salary very generous,' he went on. 'Indeed, it can only be described as extremely modest.'

She tilted her head in assent.

'That's why I stressed a love of books in the advertisement,' he said. 'I thought it might be a good way of passing the time for some young person, someone with a fondness for literature.'

She nodded and made as if to rise.

'Please,' he said quickly, going up to the chair and staying her with a wave of the hand. 'You mustn't misunderstand me. It's not an elaborate way of telling you to go. I'm only trying to make the position clear to you.'

She settled herself back into the chair.

'I take it you're fond of books?'

'I don't know if it answers your question,' she said, her arm rising in that already familiar warding-off movement, 'but, as it happens, I have a degree in English Literature.'

He stared at her.

'From the University of Cuyama,' she added. 'I graduated

27

last year.' The faintest suggestion of a smile livened her face. 'I can, if you wish, show you my graduation certificate.' She glanced down at the handbag on her lap. 'I have it here with me.'

'A degree in English Literature and you want to come here and work as my assistant!' He threw up his arms. 'Forgive me for saying so – but it doesn't make sense.'

She blinked out towards the peeling billboards.

'With a degree in English Literature – and I'm sure I don't have to tell you this – you must be able to get a dozen jobs. Not in my wildest dreams did I expect any of my applicants to be equipped with degrees in English Literature. You could be a teacher. Cuyama is crying out for teachers.'

'I don't want to be a teacher.'

This declaration, evenly delivered, surprised him nearly as much as the announcement that she possessed a degree.

'But why not? What's wrong with being a teacher?'

She did not answer.

'You'll be bored working here,' he said, gazing at her in growing bewilderment. 'It'll be a waste of your talents, of all those years of study. Don't you see that?' He resumed his pacing. 'Of course the job is yours if you want it. That goes without saying. Only . . .'

'When can I start?'

'Tomorrow, if you like. Any time.'

It was agreed she would start work on the following day.

She rose from the chair, looping her handbag over her shoulder.

'An assistant with a degree in English Literature!' He wagged his head at her.

She put on her dark glasses. At the doorway she halted. She seemed to want to say something. Abruptly, with a quick little shrug, she turned away and hurried down the steps.

'Until tomorrow,' he said.

She did not reply. Perhaps she had not heard.

He watched her walk down the fissured path and step out on to the pavement. He watched her cross the main road, incandescent in the morning light, and stand under the peeling billboards of the cinema. He watched her flag down a cruising taxi. He waved as she got in. But she was not looking at him or at the bookshop and there was no acknowledgement.

The following day she arrived and took up her station on the stool which was placed near the entrance.

*

'I've found the most extraordinary person to help me out in the bookshop,' Aubrey told his mother. He was too full of his news to be as discreet as he would have liked.

Stephanie St Pierre bent on him a suspicious stare. Reference to the Aurora usually had this effect on her. This first insinuation of Dina's name into the St Pierre household had not been auspicious.

'If she has a degree why is she applying for the job?' Stephanie asked.

'That's exactly what I asked her.'

'What did she say?'

What indeed had she said? Reviewing their encounter, he realised that she had, in fact, said very little. 'She's still in the process of finding out what she would really like to do with her life,' he said. 'After all, she only graduated last year.' Instinctively, he withheld her disavowal of a teaching career. In a sense, he withheld it even from himself. Already, he had begun to invent a character for her; to clothe with plausible interpretation the areas of obscurity.

'I don't like the sound of this,' Stephanie said. 'You were never a good judge of character.' Jewelled index finger playing about the corners of her mouth, Stephanie St Pierre had gazed sourly at her son.

*

29

Aubrey had spoken truly: there was very little to do in the bookshop. Business was virtually non-existent in the mornings when the becalmed Aurora was sunk in a cloistered quietude behind its wire enclosure. Aubrey retired to the room at the back of the shop – still smelling faintly of the medicines the previous tenant had stored there – where he clacked intermittently at his ageing office typewriter. At intervals he would wander out into the shop, hands plunged into the spacious pockets of his smock. The odd browser might make an appearance, browse bemusedly and go away. For most of them the bookshop provided a temporary haven from the scorching sun. Dina, according to instructions, kept an eye on them to see that nothing was pilfered – though she had no idea what she was meant to do if she should spot a thief. It was only in the last hour or two of the business day that the Aurora stood a reasonable chance of selling anything. However, Aubrey stuck rigidly to the schedule he had set himself.

'Have we sold anything so far today?' he would ask as he closed and bolted the doors at lunch time – when the shop closed for an hour.

Dina would shake her head. 'Nothing.'

The question was repeated when he brought her a cup of tea at four o'clock.

Dina would shake her head. 'Only a browser so far.'

Sometimes, not more than half a dozen books – and these chiefly paperbacks – were sold in a week. The Aurora's lack of success was so conspicuous that she could not help marvelling at its existence. However, she suspected it was a subject Aubrey would not have cared for her to bring up. Reference to something so obvious would have been not merely unnecessary but tasteless and embarrassing. It would have been like drawing to the attention of its possessor a physical deformity of which he himself must be only too painfully aware. Thus a kind of taboo hung over discussion of the bookshop's performance. If Aubrey had misgivings, he betrayed no sign of them to her; while Dina, having given her usual answers to his formal queries about sales, either relapsed into silence or went on to talk of other matters. But regard for his sensibilities did not entirely account for her reticence. At bottom, the bookshop's success or lack of success was of no concern to her. The Aurora was Aubrey's affair. Her purposes and its purposes coincided only tangentially; no more, in fact, than did those of the browsers who used it as a convenient shelter from the sun.

There were others apart from the browsers, for whom the bookshop provided a sanctuary of another kind: the stupefied strays from the Serenity Bar who seemed irresistibly drawn to its cloistered quiet. They would crawl in among the pillars beneath the building and curl themselves to sleep. Some would spend the night there, emerging dusty and red-eyed at unpredictable intervals during the course of the morning and stumbling out towards the pavement. Others would squat stubbornly on the eave-shaded steps and refuse to move, alternately bursting into snatches of song, swearing at invisible enemies and muttering to themselves.

One day a squatter exposed himself to her. It took Dina a few seconds to realise what was happening. When she did, she screamed. Aubrey came running into the shop. Dina pointed wordlessly at the man who was now giggling and swaying on the steps, in imminent danger of toppling over. He was still – her gaze returned helplessly to the offending region – clutching his naked member as if it assisted him in maintaining his precarious balance.

Aubrey grabbed the man by the shoulders as much to restrain him as to prevent him from falling over. He coaxed and chivvied. 'You go home and sleep it off, my good fellow. Look at you! You can hardly stand straight. Sleep will make you feel a lot better.'

Dina stared at the man. He was a wasted old Hindustani of indeterminate age. His shrunken body was encased in a bag of slack skin, wrinkling into loose folds at the joints.

31

Most strikingly, his arms and legs appeared to be not much thicker – the comparison came of its own accord – than the purple protuberance he had flourished at her. It was the plumpest, healthiest part of him. What remained of his vitality had been sucked into it.

Aubrey guided the man down the steps and escorted him to the gate. He watched him stagger the first few steps along the pavement before returning inside.

'Are you all right?' he asked.

She smiled past him, waving away his solicitude.

'One more lost soul,' Aubrey said. 'We must never be too quick to condemn. We must always show compassion.'

Neither referred to the incident again.

She also had to contend with the beggars. They were young and old, male and female, maimed and whole. Some came singly, others in small groups. With them too Aubrey was gentle and showed compassion. But this did not lead to a prodigal scattering of coins since Aubrey did not believe that that kind of largesse did any good. Instead, he gave them food. This took the form of salted biscuits which he bought in quantity and stored in an air-tight drum. Some of the beggars rejected the biscuits with scorn and went away cursing. Some – the majority – accepted sullenly and without thanks. Some accepted resignedly. None ever showed enthusiasm. As Aubrey's assistant, it fell to her to dole out these biscuits.

She was awkward in the philanthropic role Aubrey had assigned her: she had always turned a blind eye to the city's beggar population, brushing aside the entreating arms or stumps of arms waved in her face as she brushed aside the plaguing flies that attempted to settle on her sweating skin. Having hurriedly and ungraciously doled out the biscuits, she would shoo the recipients out to the pavement. 'Out! Out!' she hissed, keeping her voice down so that Aubrey would not hear her. She hated the whining self-abasement; was revolted by the festering sores they displayed like badges of merit. She cringed when the smaller children tugged at the hem of her skirt and touched her. She developed the irrational fear that they might transmit to her the diseases they harboured. So, if she had been touched, she would surreptitiously wash those parts of herself that had been contaminated by contact with them, telling herself all the while that she was being ridiculous. All the same, when Aubrey was not there, she seized the opportunity to lock the gate and bar them all access.

There were the browsers, the drunks, the beggars; and, there were Aubrey's friends. Some of these would actually buy books – though, as Dina noticed, they usually did so on credit. Aubrey seemed to enjoy drawing their attention to her.

'I have the great privilege,' he would say, pointing at her, 'of employing an assistant with a degree in English Literature. What do you think of that?'

These well-meaning but clumsy attempts to compliment her and advertise her presence disconcerted Dina. She felt exceedingly foolish, unable to utter a word in response. It was as if she were doing the boasting herself and Aubrey was simply her mouthpiece. Pretending not to have heard, she would bury her face in a book.

As it was, most of Aubrey's friends – and this, in its way, was no less disconcerting – appeared not to think anything in particular of her having a degree in English Literature. Those who did not studiously ignore the disclosure only smiled patronisingly before continuing to scour the shelves. One or two had even reacted with a touch of hostility. A tall, reedy young man with bulbous eyes, a sharp wedge of a nose and shoulder-length hair had giggled and said: 'What a lucky man you are, Aubrey, to have installed such a prodigy on the premises. I see I must take extra-special care in choosing the books I buy from you. I wouldn't want your assistant to disapprove of my taste.'

Afterwards Aubrey said, 'Malcolm is one of our more

talented younger poets. You should read his work.'

'I wish you wouldn't tell your friends I have a degree,' she said.

'Why not?' Aubrey replied. 'Why hide your light under a bushel? It's something you should be proud of.'

Dina had almost stamped her foot in vexation. 'I'd rather you didn't,' she said.

From then on Aubrey desisted.

She would sit quietly at her desk reading or doodling in the margins of discarded publishers' catalogues while Aubrey clucked attentively around one or another of his distinguished customers, enunciating in his clipped, precise tones theories and opinions ranging over a wide variety of subjects. No matter what the topic, Aubrey was never at a loss for something to say. She had heard him talk with equal facility about Dutch landscape painting, Sufism and even the theory of relativity. He alternated between gaiety and solemnity, his eyes glowing with the thrill of speculation. 'With Einstein (she had heard him say) poetry and mathematics converge. I, of course, don't pretend to know anything of the higher mathematics but I do believe it's possible to have what I would call a poetic understanding of space-time. Is the Einsteinian universe really so strange after all? Is it really any more mysterious than Christianity with its three in one and one in three?'

Dina watched rather than listened to these exchanges, performed against the accompanying throb of the juke-box in the Serenity Bar. In the role of listener, Aubrey would stand or lean with one arm behind his back while with the other he stroked and twiddled his moustache. In the role of talker he would pace up and down the shop; and, if he became especially excited, he would throw out his arms in sweeping gestures. When his friends had left the shop, Aubrey would tell her who they were and what they did. They were poets, playwrights, journalists, university teachers of radical bent ... Dina lost track of the talents that

were paraded before her. 'Many of these people are bringing
to birth a new culture,' he told her. 'They're putting country
before self.'

Dina doodled as he extolled their virtues.

Late one afternoon she looked up interestedly at a woman
who ran up the steps into the shop. She was flamboyantly
dressed in a long, floral-patterned skirt which swirled about
her ankles. The tips of a pair of suede boots, pale green in
colour, flashed out from under the hem of the skirt. A
short-sleeved blouse of crushed velvet dipped low over her
bosom. Tangled hair sprawled across her shoulders. A string
of black and lilac beads dangled from her neck. Her lips
were cherry-red and an opalescent sheen glistened on her
eyelids. She smoked acrid-smelling cigarettes (Dina saw
from the pack that they were an exotic French brand) using
an ivory holder, puffing clouds of smoke at Aubrey. At one
point the cigarette slipped from its holder, grazing her skirt
as it fell to the floor.

'Fuck!' She pivoted sharply on the heels of her boots,
brushing the ash off her skirt. 'Fuck!' Then she raised her
head and saw Dina staring at her. She laughed. 'My bad
language has shocked your assistant rigid,' she said to
Aubrey, who did not seem to be altogether pleased.

Presently, Aubrey came over to where she sat. 'Will you
wrap these for Mrs Henderson?' He placed before her three
volumes of Proust.

'Cash or ...'

'On account,' Mrs Henderson intervened. 'I have all my
books on account.'

'Who is Mrs Henderson?' Dina asked afterwards. This
was the first time she had taken the initiative in eliciting
information about his friends.

'Beatrice is my first cousin,' Aubrey said. He frowned. 'As
you see, she's terribly avant-garde. Too much so for my
simpler tastes.'

Nevertheless, there were long periods when she had to

deal neither with browsers, nor drunks, nor beggars, nor Aubrey's friends; when all she did was sit on her stool and stare at the cinema posters and traffic and listen to the steady thump of the juke-box in the Serenity Bar. The little gold watch on her wrist ticked away the minutes and hours of the day. But the time it measured was circular: as circular as the dial round whose face the tiny hands tirelessly rotated. It could have been the same day, the same hour, the same minute, that was being endlessly repeated. The cars and lorries went by; the Serenity Bar hummed and throbbed; the afternoon bloomed into incandescence; the hands of the gold watch toiled round its treadmill. Like a stream that divides itself to flow around an obstacle, so time seemed to divide itself and flow around her as she perched somnolently on her stool.

'It must be so boring for you,' Aubrey said.

'I'm not bored,' she replied.

'But to sit here day after day, with so little to do ... it seems such a waste of your potential.'

'It's preferable to sitting at home and wasting my potential there,' she answered.

He smiled. Shaking his head at her, he returned to the back room.

Another time he said: 'If you ever wish to leave, you mustn't hesitate to say so. You mustn't feel any false sense of obligation to me.'

'I have no wish to leave.' She brooded. 'You shouldn't worry so much about me.'

'I feel so guilty about keeping you here.'

She laughed. 'You're not keeping me here. I'm keeping myself here. I'm here of my own free will.'

'Why do you find teaching so off-putting a profession?' he asked on yet another occasion. That disavowal had never ceased to trouble him. 'After all, your father was a teacher.'

She blinked out into the golden glare, raising her arm in

that warding-off gesture. 'Perhaps that's why,' she replied, and would say no more.

She began to be afraid that Aubrey's conscience might get the better of him and that, from the most laudable of motives, he might take it into his head to send her away; or that he might decide that having an assistant was a luxury he could ill afford; or even that the Aurora would go out of business. What would become of her then? Without the bookshop she would have only her room and the narrow veranda at home with its baskets of plants. A note of urgency crept into her constantly reiterated assurances that she was not bored; not wasting her imagined talents.

It was good to wake in the morning and remember that she had somewhere to go and something to do. To prolong and heighten the sensation, she deliberately delayed getting out of bed so that she was forced to rush if she was to arrive at the bookshop on time. She like entering the welcoming coolness of the Aurora and inhaling the bookish odours that greeted her as she stepped inside. She liked exchanging the first polite pleasantries of the day with Aubrey. She liked settling herself on her stool in the corner by the entrance. She was almost happy. Only the cinema posters, constantly changing, would occasionally jolt her into an awareness of time inexorably creeping forward and carrying her along with it. Looking at the posters, she would suddenly recall a luridly depicted scene or face and reflect, with a slowly dawning wonder, that between it and the lurid scene now decorating the billboards several others had intervened.

In his anxiety to stave off boredom and his eagerness to instruct her, Aubrey had recommended that she read some of his favourite nineteenth-century Russian authors. He had gone round the shelves, made a selection and presented them to her.

'Do read these,' he urged. 'You'll find they penetrate to the heart of the human condition. The problems they deal with are universal.'

Dina was not averse to the idea of becoming acquainted with those great works. Seeing Aubrey's friends, half-listening to their erudite chatter, had had an effect on her. She was prodded into an uneasy consciousness of the gaps in her reading. But when she tried to read the novels Aubrey had given her the words danced on the page and her attention wandered to the cinema posters. The impulsion to fill in the gaps in her knowledge remained notional.

'How are you getting on with the Russians?' Aubrey asked.

'I'm a slow reader,' she said.

Aubrey's eyes dilated approvingly. 'I'm glad to hear that,' he said. 'I read slowly too. Great books are like great wines. You don't gulp down a great wine. You roll it on the tongue, you savour the bouquet.'

Dina, who knew nothing about great wines, said nothing. He smiled encouragingly and returned to the back room.

Aubrey's typewriter clacked spasmodically between prolonged intervals of silence. Dina would listen to him pacing the study: only an insubstantial wooden partition separated them. Once she heard him groan aloud. Sometimes he wandered into the shop, hands in pockets, forehead puckered, eyes glazed and reddened by strain. He would walk up and down, staring at the rows of books. Every so often he stopped, pulled one out and read briefly from it before returning it to its place with a small, sad shake of the head. Then he would go and stand in the doorway, looking out at the traffic. Dina did not know the nature of the struggle being waged in the back room. He had never spoken about it to her and she had not bothered to ask. The intermittent clack of his typewriter merely added to the somnolent atmosphere of the shop. She questioned its purpose no more than she questioned the purpose of the drunken hum that emanated from the Serenity Bar.

One afternoon, after chasing away a drunk who had been squatting on the steps, she turned round to see Aubrey perched on her stool.

'Have you ever tried to write?' he asked.

'No,' she said, gazing wildly at him. 'Never.'

His rounded, liquid eyes darkened a shade. 'Until you try it for yourself you can't begin to know the agony involved in the creative process. The effort! The pain! It's like wringing blood out of a stone.'

'Are you writing something?' She looked at him stupidly.

'I'm trying to write a novel,' he said after a while. 'The trouble is that it might all prove to be wasted labour. It's possible that I don't have the talent for the task I've set myself.'

Dina had no idea what – if anything – was expected of her. No ready-made phrases of consolation leapt to her lips. Not being versed in the art of giving sympathy, she continued to gaze wildly at him.

'Shall I give you some idea of what I'm trying to do?' he asked.

'If you'd like.'

He began to pace about the shop, addressing himself to the ranks of books. 'Imagine a family – a family, if you wish, like my own. Two hundred years ago we were slave-owners. We considered ourselves aristocrats, born rulers of men. My aim is to depict the evolution of this family and the society of which they formed part. One part of the book will describe the family as it is now. The other will tell of the family as it was then. These two stories will alternate. On the one hand, there'll be the family with its plantations, its pictures and furniture imported from London and Paris, living in constant apprehension of slave revolt, resorting to sadism at the slightest sign of disobedience. On the other hand, you'll have its descendants as they are today, living in reduced circumstances, but their safety no less threatened than it was two hundred years ago. The two stories do not simply alternate but begin to coalesce. The past is contained in the present and the present is contained in the past. They become, as the book reaches its climax, one story, one torrent of historical experience . . . do you get the idea? It's not a costume drama, not a tropical *Gone With The Wind*.' He smiled. 'In Cuyama the Scarlett O'Haras brandished whips and cut off the breasts of slave women they feared might prove too attractive to their husbands.' He pulled dispiritedly at his meagre beard. 'Would you like to read a little of what I've written? It's all very rough, of course – only a first draft.'

'I'm not sure I'd be a good judge. I . . .' There was a touch of something like panic in her reaction.

'Why shouldn't you be a good judge?'

He went through to the back room and returned with a few pages of typescript. She seemed afraid of touching the white sheets he held out to her.

'You must be completely honest with me,' he said. 'If it's trash you must say so.'

She read the typescript that evening. As she read, she seemed to hear the agonised tap-tap of the typewriter in the back room. She returned it to him the next day. He looked at her expectantly.

'Interesting,' she said. It was the best she could manage.

Aubrey did not press her. Concealing his disappointment, he returned to the medicinal odours of the back room.

Not many days after this, as she was idly looking along the shelves, she saw Flaubert's *Madame Bovary*. She added it to her stockpile of Russians.

'Flaubert,' Aubrey said. 'Are you reading him?'

'No. I was just glancing through it.' She brushed imaginary strands of her hair away from her eyes. 'I read it a long time ago. I wanted to refresh my memory.'

'It's a good thing to do,' Aubrey said. 'One forgets so much.' He riffled the pages. 'I read it a long time ago too. I remember feeling rather sorry for her husband.'

'For him!' The exclamation was involuntary.

Aubrey looked at her.

Dina collected herself. 'What I mean is that I remember feeling more sorry for her than for him.'

'Her end could hardly have been more tragic, I agree.' He read desultorily. 'But her husband – Charles – he suffered greatly too. Her betrayal killed him in the end, didn't it?'

'I don't remember.'

'I believe it did. Our actions don't happen in a vacuum.' He smiled at her. 'We're all each other's hostages, aren't we?'

Dina did not answer.

'What a sad, deluded creature she was.' Aubrey wagged his head. 'She'd stuffed her head with foolish romantic notions.'

'You think it's foolish to be a romantic?' Dina asked.

'If it goes against the facts of life, it's more than foolish. It then becomes a form of suicide.' Aubrey folded his arms across his chest, gazing down at her. 'We must be able to distinguish the possible from the impossible.'

'Doesn't this bookshop go against the facts of life – the facts of Cuyamese life?'

'I expect, looked at from a certain point of view, it does.' Aubrey stroked his moustache. 'But I try to recognise limits. I know I can't fly. I know I can't defy gravity without injuring myself.'

'How does one discover what the limits are? How does one distinguish the possible from the impossible?'

'Through a combination of reason, experience and common sense.'

'What are called the facts of life can be a prison. Don't you agree?' She readjusted herself on the stool. 'What, for instance, do the facts of life in a place like Cuyama amount to? We're tethered on a very short rope. We're allowed so little.'

He contemplated her pensively. 'Therefore we must bend our efforts to lengthening that rope so that we aren't hauled back at every step. We all have a part to play in that process.'

'You mean you'd have me become a teacher!' She man-

aged a pale burst of laughter. 'It always comes back to that.
Is that what you'd have suggested to Emma Bovary?' The
pale laughter was shadowed by a paler mockery. She had a
vision of her father, his fingers stained with chalk-dust,
stalking the school-room; she saw the red-eyed boys emerging at twilight, slinking away with their dog-eared textbooks
in the gathering darkness. She laughed. 'If we Cuyamese
had enough rope and if we could honestly face up to the
facts, we'd hang ourselves.'

Often they would have lunch together, sitting out on the
steps at the rear of the bookshop. They looked out on a
garden of tangled shrubbery and sun-scorched grass lazily
tended by Albert, the boy whom Aubrey had hired to do the
necessary weeding and watering. He wandered around the
garden in a faded cotton shirt and a pair of khaki trousers so
frayed at the seat that the smooth black skin of his buttocks
showed through the lattice-work of threads. Beyond the
wooden back fence, amidst a grove of plantain, mango and
breadfruit trees, was the colony of hovels from which Albert
emerged to perform his duties.

Plates resting on their knees, Dina would eat sandwiches
while Aubrey, who had pretensions to vegetarianism, ate
chaste salads and boiled eggs. Aubrey, as was his wont,
would talk randomly, executing a variety of gestures with his
fork; and Dina, as was her wont, would pay only sporadic
attention to the things he said. Lulled by the heat, she would
follow Albert's sleepy movements about the garden and
stare at the people who passed along the street that ran
along one side of the bookshop.

*

One Thursday afternoon – the bookshop closed early on
Thursdays – he invited her to accompany him on one of his
philanthropic excursions to the Charlestown slums. Reck-
lessly, she agreed. She spent the afternoon trailing in his
wake through the terraced lower slopes of the hills rising

above Charlestown. Aubrey quickly gathered about him a following of near-naked urchins with the bloom of dust on their grape-black skins; with the livid wounds of festering sores glowing like nebulae on arms and legs; with protuberant navels projecting like misshapen thumbs from swollen bellies. He moved among them with an easy familiarity, caressing tangled heads, doling out biscuits from the big brown paper bag he always carried with him on these expeditions. Every so often he looked back at her over his shoulder and smiled encouragingly.

She watched from a distance as he paid calls on old women, stiffened by privation and arthritic frailty; she stood on rickety doorsteps and stared into darkened interiors animated by the dim movements of men and women whose faces she could not see; she listened to him offering advice. He was indefatigable. The urchins tugged at her skirt and extended cupped palms. Below them was the desert expanse of Independence Park and the grey plain of the harbour enclosed by its pair of misty headlands.

Afterwards, they had a drink at the Park Hotel. Sitting on cushioned cane chairs in the air-conditioned gloom, they sipped the rum punches Aubrey had ordered. She stirred her glass with a plastic stick adorned with an emblematic palm tree.

'What makes you do it?' she asked. 'Is it only because two hundred years ago your family were slave owners?'

'Yes.'

'That really does prey on your conscience?' She sounded sceptical.

'I feel I owe these people something ' he said. 'Without the compelled labours of their forefathers families like mine could never have existed. It isn't a complex point of view.' He gazed up to the mirror behind the bar where the rows of bottles were reflected. 'Do you think it's ridiculous to be conscience-stricken?'

'I don't know. How could I possibly know?' She laughed,

gesturing helplessly. 'I can't imagine what it's like to have slave-owning ancestors. I come out of darkness, out of blankness. I have no past.' She was suddenly restless. 'I ought to be going. My parents must be wondering where I am.'

'I'll run you back,' he said.

'Don't do that.' She seemed alarmed. 'I can easily find myself a taxi. Stay and finish your drink.' She pointed at his half-empty glass.

Despite her protestations, he insisted. During the drive, she held herself tensely erect and separate from him, discouraging his attempts at conversation. She directed him to a modest wooden house set close to the pavement and hemmed in by its neighbours. Fretted eaves fringed an unlit veranda hung with plants in wire baskets. Light glowed milkily beyond a half-opened front door veiled by lace curtains. On the veranda a man sat on a rocking-chair. He leaned forward, peering at the car.

'Is that you, Dina?' The man had an invalid's querulous voice. He made no move to rise from the rocking-chair, merely leaning forward, peering blindly into the street.

'Yes, Papa.'

Someone else – her mother perhaps – appeared behind the lace curtains. Dina ran up the few steps to the darkened veranda and was swiftly swallowed up in the milky obscurity glowing behind the lace curtains.

*

It was about a fortnight after this that they had returned to the plush, air-conditioned gloom of the Park Hotel and sat once more on the cushioned cane chairs, stirring their drinks with the plastic sticks adorned with palm-trees, looking round at the murals of leaping monkeys and flights of lime-green parrots. Aubrey, his voice mingling with the canned music, heard himself asking for her hand in marriage.

*

She did not turn up for work the next morning. Nor the morning after that. On the third day, after closing the shop, he went in search of her. He was met on the veranda by her mother, a plump, pale-skinned woman, dressed in a white cotton shift. Untidy, curling hair smoked up from the crown of her forehead. She examined him through the lace curtains. He introduced himself.

'Ah, yes,' she said, with only a marginal softening of manner. 'Mr Aubrey St Pierre.'

She parted the curtains so that he could enter. The heels of her faded, flower-embroidered slippers slapped across the floorboards. 'I'll go and tell her you're here. Take a seat.' Mrs Mallingham disappeared with a decisive slapping of her slippers through another lace-curtained doorway.

Aubrey, left alone, took the opportunity to examine the room. He noted the dull lustre of the floorboards, the framed family photographs lining the walls, the effigy above the front door of Christ on the Cross; he noted the small, glass-doored cabinet arrayed with modest pieces of silver and crystal and china-ware; he noted the bookcase with its dusty volumes of the English classics, ageing text-books and back numbers of the *Reader's Digest*; he noted the upright piano, its top spread with a red cloth on which stood a blue-eyed doll dressed in a crinolined skirt gaily braided with ribbons of many colours – the piano, he suspected, had not been used for a long time; he noted the mahogany dining-table, in the centre of which was a tall vase filled with artificial flowers, the blooms of more temperate zones, bleached by tropical light and heat – the table too looked as if it had not been used for a long time; he noted the studio portrait of a youthful, slimmer Mrs Mallingham, face in soft focus, curling hair rippling lushly against her cheeks ... he noted the furniture, arm-rests darkened with use and polish, fraying coverings washed into colourless attenuation. He understood that it had been a room painfully created and maintained but now given over to exhaustion, surrendered to decay. Looking at it, some of the obscurity surrounding his assistant lifted. He was moved in a new way by her.

Dina arrived, pushing her way through the lace curtains.

*

They drove to the promenade down by the harbour. They strolled along the sea wall, seeking the shade of the twisted trees planted down the middle of the promenade. A cooling wind blew off the water. They stopped near the remains of a wooden jetty. She leaned against the sea wall, digging her fingernails into the blackened balustrade. During especially high tides, the brimming swell exploded into cannonades of smoky spray that washed on to the road. As a child, she used to run the gauntlet of these spectacular cannonades, returning home soaked and scalded by the salty spray.

That day, however, the sea was calm. Bubbling and frothing, the discoloured waves hissed up the narrow strip of shingly beach, shuffling and shunting the pebbles. They foamed and forked round the larger moss-covered rocks. Here and there tiny crabs, skirting the flush of the water, scuttled among tangled nests of seaweed whose rankness tainted the air. Pieces of wood, crates, bottles, coconut shells, bobbed on the oil-stained swell. A quarrelsome flock of seabirds wheeled overhead. Haze veiled the headlands enclosing the bay. She let her gaze sweep slowly along the rim of the empty horizon, traversing the headland to her right, lingering on the just visible ruins of the fort that had once guarded the entrance to the harbour.

At night, when the strings of coloured bulbs glowed and the food vendors arrived with their carts and lit their smoky flambeaux, when the lights of the city traced the curve of the bay and spread like a rash on the hills behind it, when the sky was lit by an electric radiance and the harbour sparkled with reflection, the promenade acquired a spurious gaiety. It became crowded with people out for a breath of fresh air. Old ladies with shawls wrapped around their shoulders sat

on the benches. The young perched on the sea wall. Court-
ing couples, arms curled round each other's waists, paraded,
stopping from time to time to stare out over the water. What
adventure was promised! But she had learned a long time
ago that there was no adventure to be had there. That was
an illusion provoked by the artificial radiance of the sky, the
smoking flambeaux of the food stalls, the strings of coloured
bulbs. Convincing to the credulous eyes of the child, the
scene acquired the immobility of a painted backdrop in the
eye of the adult sensitive to its sameness.

'I'm not suitable.' she said.

'You mustn't be too sure of that.'

'I'm sterile,' she said. She turned and looked at him. 'I'm
barren – not biologically, perhaps, but in every other way.
Of what conceivable use could I be?'

He reached forward and touched her arm.

'You've taken pity on me,' she said. 'You shouldn't have
done that. You pity me as you pity those children up there.'
Looking away from the water, she indicated the terraced
hills rising beyond the jumble of rooftops. 'You wish to
rescue me as you wish to rescue them. You wish to save me
from myself as you wish to save them from themselves. You
believe something can be made of me. You want to prevent
the waste of a BA. Isn't that so?'

This was another of the frames he most often froze and
reflected upon. He had lacked the courage to concede there
was truth in what she said. Not the whole truth. Nor the
truth as he would have described it. He would have liked to
explain that the compassion he felt for her – and the tender
pity to which it gave rise – were for him indistinguishable
from what was commonly called love. He would have liked
to explain that he was not capable of loving in any other
way. For, if compassion and tender pity did not create love –
what did? If they weren't good enough – what was? There
were, no doubt, other ways of loving; but they were beyond
his reach. One person's love for another, he would have

47

liked to tell her, is always unique. People can only do what they can; be what they are.

'You misunderstand me,' he had said.

She had looked away from him and the terraced hills, blinking out across the oily swell of the harbour.

'I'm not suitable,' she said.

'Let me be the judge of that,' he urged.

'You will grow to hate me,' she said.

He touched her arm again and saw that she was crying.

A month later, amid the wood-panelled splendours of the Registry Office, they were married.

Chapter Four

When she opened her eyes the curtains were flushed with sunlight. Aubrey was already out of bed, having his morning shower. Staring at the light-soaked curtains, she recalled the dream out of which she had been roused. She had been wandering in a dank garden, heavy with the musky scents of exotic blooms. She was searching for the child who, a moment before, had been walking along beside her. But the child was nowhere to be seen. She had broken into a trot, then had started to run, calling out, slipping and stumbling on the meandering paths coated with moss. The garden had become wilder and wilder, its paths submerged in the tangled undergrowth, until it was no longer a garden but more like a jungle. Abruptly, the child reappeared in front of her, waving her forward. 'Look at what I found,' Clara said. Glancing down, she saw that Clara had uncovered a corpse. She recognised herself, sprawled naked in the undergrowth. Her skin was caked with mud, her hair was encrusted with withered moss and there were holes where her eyes had been. Silently, she had gazed upon herself. At that point, she had woken up.

She listened to the streaming gush of the shower. Aubrey grunted as he slapped and massaged his flesh. Her head aching, Dina stared at the fiery curtains. Aubrey emerged from the bathroom wrapped in a blue-striped robe, his hair and wispy beard glinting with droplets of water. He went to the bed and looked down at her.

'You look tired,' he said, scrubbing his hair with a towel. 'Didn't you sleep well?'

She closed her eyes, concentrating on the gliding amoebic shapes patterning the screen of her eyelids. 'It was too hot,' she said. A droplet splashed on her forehead, cool on the warm skin.

He went across the room, pulled open the curtains and looked up at the sky – blue, cloudless, but already veiled with a film of haze. 'We need some rain,' he said. 'Some thunder and lightning.'

She offered no comment.

He came back to her. 'Do you have a headache?'

'No.' A flicker of irritation tightened her face.

Desisting from further questioning, he embarked on his daily programme of exercises. He touched his toes, arched and swayed his back, did push-ups; he contorted his body in half a dozen different poses. Lately, he had added jogging to his repertoire. Two or three times a week, after sundown, he would push his slim frame round the asphalted perimeter of Independence Park.

She waited until he had dressed and left the room before she opened her eyes again. Effortfully, she swung herself out of bed. Her limbs felt leaden; her eyelids were puffed. She scowled at the unprepossessing reflection the mirror returned to her. How drawn she looked! How pale! How bruised and dark the skin under her eyes! She ran a finger along her collar-bone. It seemed to be more prominent than ever. Could she still be considered pretty? She stared hard at herself. For as long as she could remember her prettiness had been universally acknowledged; always she had been the most praised and admired of the sisters. She was the one who most closely resembled her mother in feature. The idea of crawling back into bed and pulling the sheet over her head was tempting. However, she decided to resist the temptation. That would only have quickened Aubrey's solicitude; and she was in no mood to endure that. Wearily she showered and dressed and made her way downstairs.

*

50

Aubrey was sitting on the back veranda. The wire baskets –
containing orchids and ferns – suspended from the eaves
were still dripping from their recent watering. Aubrey was
methodically working his way through his breakfast. 'Breakfast,' he had assured her time and again, 'is the most important meal of the day. You must make sure you have a good
breakfast even if you don't feel like it.' And there he was,
practising what he preached while he read the newspaper.
She took her accustomed place at the white-painted
wrought-iron table dutifully arrayed with table-mats, paper
napkins and indifferently washed items of stainless steel cutlery.

The slatternly Selma, with Clara perched on her hip,
produced a glass of orange juice, some thin, half-charred
slices of toast and a boiled egg whose shell had fractured.
Seepages of water-logged albumen protruded like warts
from the fissures. There was no butter because the shops had
none to sell; and there was no jam for the same reason. In
another two weeks there might, with luck, be butter and
jam. But, as was more than likely, their reappearance would
coincide with the disappearance of bread and coffee from
the shelves. That was how it went and you became accustomed. She had heard from Aubrey that the International
Monetary Fund looked upon the Cuyamese as lepers; that
its animosity resulted in a chronic lack of foreign exchange;
and that this chronic shortage meant bare shelves in the
shops. She did not understand everything he told her and did
not really try to. It seemed unnecessary to do so.

She surveyed her sabotaged breakfast without appetite,
then scanned the headlines of the newspaper Aubrey was
reading. It was taken up with the usual stuff: the more or less
statutory photograph of the President (garbed in the lushly
braided, richly medallioned uniform of a general, he was
shown inspecting a detachment of girl cadets) and reports of
speeches by assorted ministers. She looked out into the little
garden with its solitary orange tree, its weedy bed of rose

51

bushes, its shrubbery of hibiscus, bougainvillaea and croton. Her gaze roamed over the balding lawn of crabgrass, settling on the bleached deck-chair in which she often read and dozed. At this hour of the morning the garden lay in shade. Towards mid-morning, the sun would begin to creep over it. At two o'clock it would be drowned in heat and light. By five, it would begin to cool again as the shadow thrown by the house lengthened across it. She watched the iridescent flutter of a pair of humming birds feeding on the pink and white blossom of the bleeding-heart vine covering the wooden fence. She wondered if the card was still lying in the gutter. At some point she must venture out there and have a look.

Aubrey's voice broke into her abstraction. It was his habit to comment on the morning's news and, if he was particularly outraged or excited by something, to read aloud entire passages to her.

'They're talking again of introducing curbs on the press,' he said, taking a sip of coffee. 'Just listen to this.' He began reading aloud to her. ' "The time has come for us to redefine the priorities and goals of the development process and of national reconstruction. The imperialists and their home-grown lackeys ..." ' He looked out from behind the newspaper. 'See what people like myself have become. Home-grown lackeys!' He laughed good-naturedly. Dina tried her best to seem receptive. He went on reading. ' "The imperialists and their home-grown lackeys enjoy lecturing us on the virtues and benefits of a so-called free press and a so-called free exchange of ideas. They write letters to the imperialist press complaining about us. We are called thugs and gangsters and hijackers ..." ' Aubrey lowered the newspaper. 'Can you,' he asked, 'imagine a fairer, more objective characterisation?' She did her best to seem amused. He went on reading. ' "Because we are not afraid, we have let them publish their slanders here and abroad. But their time is fast running out. Have we struggled and bled for our freedom

52

only in order to have the wool pulled over our eyes?'' Yes!'
Aubrey exclaimed. 'Yes! Yes!' In his excitement, he
pounded the table with his fist, causing the cutlery to rattle.
He went on reading. ' "I say No! Your Comrade President
says No! You, the people, say No! We must have a press
that reflects our ideals and our values. We will not tolerate
subversion either by deed or word after you, the people,
have spoken. We will not tolerate negativity ..." '

Dina watched the humming birds.

Selma reappeared. She began clearing away the remains
of Aubrey's breakfast. He folded the newspaper and rested
it on the table.

'You haven't eaten a thing,' Aubrey examined her face
with concern.

'I'm not hungry.'

'You really should eat something.'

'I told you – I'm not hungry.' She spoke more sharply
than she had intended.

'That journalist friend of yours,' she said, 'the Englishman ... I forget his name ...'

'Alex,' Aubrey said, wrinkling his forehead at her. 'Alexander Richer.'

'He arrives today, doesn't he?'

'Yes. I'm meeting him at the airport.' He looked at his
watch. 'Would you like to come for the drive?'

'You're planning to bring him here for lunch, aren't
you?' She regarded him listlessly.

'If that's all right with you.'

'That's all right with me. But, in that case, I'd better stay
here – make sure everything's in order.' She flicked crumbs
off the table. 'How long did you say he was staying?'

'Two or three days at the most. It's really only a stop-
over.'

Her mouth distended itself into the semblance of a smile.
'A stopover ... well, I don't suppose we're worth any more
than that.' She continued to flick crumbs off the table.

'It all counts,' Aubrey said. 'Look.' He pointed towards the orange-tree.

Swivelling, Dina glimpsed a flash of yellow and black among the branches.

Aubrey left the table. Dina went into the garden. Going to the fence, she plucked a handful of blossom from the bleeding-heart vine. A burst of high-pitched twittering came from the orange-tree. She watched the restless flutter of yellow and black among the leaves. Unthinkingly she crushed the blossoms she was holding, scattering them on the grass. A little later she wandered out into the street. The card had gone. Where it had been a trickle of brown water flowed, sparkling in the sunlight.

*

Some weeks before, the People's Plebiscite – as it was called – had been announced. It was Cuyama's big news. Indeed, it was its only news. The announcement had sent shockwaves of terror and counter-shockwaves of fanaticism rumbling through the society. It dominated Aubrey's waking hours – he seemed to think of little else. It dominated the conversation of all their friends. Petitions had been circulated. Manifestos had been composed. Protest marches were planned. Protest meetings were held. Letters, festooned with signatures, had been written to *The Times* in London, the *New York Times* and a dozen other publications of note. Aubrey's name appeared on many of these effusions which were saturated with outrage and the delineation of constitutional niceties.

'We, the undersigned, citizens from all walks of life, consider it our duty to draw the world's attention to the gross violation of human rights which, under the smokescreen of Constitutional Reform, is about to be unleashed ...' etc, etc.

Aubrey had taken a hand in the composition of some of these documents. To Dina he read aloud the drafts he had composed at his cluttered desk in the bookshop. 'What do you think?' he would ask. 'Is the language strong enough? Or, perhaps, too strong? One has to strike the right balance between emotion and reason. Would you say I've done that? Is my meaning clear?'

'It sounds fine,' she would invariably reply. Nevertheless, she stubbornly refused to have her own name included in the appended roll-calls. 'You'll do for both of us,' she had said. The sloganeering spawned by the Plebiscite raged out of control, a rash disfiguring the landscape with streaks of red paint the colour of blood. It could not be denied that the Plebiscite – an exercise, so the Government described it, in 'mass participatory democracy' –was, politically speaking, a most momentous business; the most dramatic happening since the coming of Independence. Then fear had rolled like a black cloud over the land and thousands had fled. Much the same thing was occurring again. The Plebiscite was the President's chosen instrument of permanently institutiona-lising himself and his party as the rulers of the country. The only way that desire could be legally enshrined was by 'rewriting' the Constitution bequeathed by the departing British: the Plebiscite would give the President 'the mass mandate of the workers and peasants who wish to rid them-selves of the last vestiges of neo-colonial dependence'.

'It must not be allowed to happen,' Aubrey had said. 'No one could be more opposed to every manifestation of neo-colonialism than I am. No one! But this so-called rewriting of the Constitution means destroying the Constitution, the taking away of our few remaining rights. It means naked dictatorship. I'm not going to sit by passively and let it happen.' The sleeves of his smock billowed with his agita-tion.

Dina had suppressed a smile. His passion, his sincerity, could not be disputed. The only thing that could be disputed was his capacity to stem the tide of events. Even Beatrice, who normally affected a high disdain for local politics, for 'the little black men who call themselves Ministers of this and Ministers of that', had been infected by the panic. She talked of 'getting the hell out of this place'.

'They are not going to lay their little black hands on me,' she said. 'No way am I going to let that happen.' Instinctively, her hand had reached up to her throat, fingering the necklace of filigreed gold gleaming there.

Dina smiled. 'What are you most anxious about, Beatie? Saving your neck or your jewellery?'

She had seen the long queues encamped daily outside the British, American and Canadian embassies. The panic showed every sign of climaxing in a stampede of the well-to-do. One day the newspaper had carried front-page photographs of these queues under the banner headline: 'With Patriots Like These Who Needs Enemies?' Reporting on the subject had been fevered, illustrated with photographs of suitcases crammed with dollar bills which had allegedly been seized by Customs officials. One item – the most scandalous of all – had shown a grinning policeman lifting the skirts of a woman, whose face was blacked out, and exhibiting a pair of gartered legs adorned with various pieces of jewellery.

When Dina next saw Beatrice (the day after the notorious photograph had appeared) she found her wan with apprehension – and, probably for the first time since Dina had come to know her –devoid of glittering ornamentation. Beatrice could hardly speak.

'It's obscene ... horrible and obscene what they did to that woman.' She shuddered, clutching at her bare throat. 'What am I to do? What are people like *us* to do? Are we to submit without a word to these humiliations, these acts of daylight robbery?' Beatrice grabbed her by the shoulders and shook her.

Dina had gently released herself and shrugged: she did not share Beatrice's obsession with jewellery. 'Listen, Beatie,' she said, in an attempt to be as sympathetic as the circumstances allowed, 'wasn't that woman damned foolish to be doing a thing like that? Shouldn't she have her head examined?'

Beatrice reacted angrily, dancing about her. 'No doubt you think I too should have my head examined for caring about my property. I keep forgetting that you and Aubrey consider yourselves to be made of finer stuff. You're patriots, socialists, lovers of the exploited people.' She waved a hand in her face. 'But don't be fooled. You may love the exploited people but they don't love you. They'll murder you in your beds, you and your idiot husband.'

This was the closest they had ever come to having an open quarrel. Beatrice seemed to be on the brink of weeping. Dina half-hoped she might: she had never seen her cry. Until then, she had always been the teacher; the woman steeped in the ways of the world, in control of every situation.

Nevertheless, Beatrice had calmed down, reverting to a plausible semblance of her confident, in-control self.

'You were right,' she said the next time they met. 'That woman was damned stupid. She brought it down on herself.' Reclining on her cane chaise-longue, she sipped from a glass of rum and water, contemplating her painted toenails. 'This business will blow over,' she observed calmly. 'They'll cool down eventually. In any case they don't frighten me.' She giggled, beckoning Dina closer. 'Look at what Ralph gave me.' Reaching into her handbag, she brought out a toy-like, matt-black firearm.

Dina had started back from the sight of it.

Beatrice's eyes sparkled; she giggled. 'You can hold it,' she said. 'It won't bite.' A peal of laughter broke from her scarlet lips.

Dina had never been in intimate contact with a gun before this. She weighed it warily in her palms. Its heaviness, its blackness, its smoothness, fascinated her. She could not take her eyes off it. 'Is it loaded?' she asked.

'Of course it's loaded, you silly child.' And again Beatrice pealed with laughter. 'What's the point of having an empty gun?'

Dina stroked the velvety metal. She had never known metal so sensuous, so thrilling, as that.

'During the day,' Beatrice said, 'I'll keep it in my hand-bag. During the night it will sleep with me under my pillow.'

Dina returned the gun to her. Even after it had left her hand she continued to feel the silky gravity of the metal. Her reaction surprised and unnerved her. She attempted to put it at a distance from her; not to think any more about it.

'You should get yourself a gun,' Beatrice said.

'We have nothing they would want,' she replied.

Beatrice resumed her contemplation of her shining toenails, sipping from her glass of rum and water.

*

Aubrey was vocal in his criticism of the exiles and would-be exiles. He had had heated arguments with Beatrice and Ralph on the subject.

'It's cowardly to run away,' he had said to the latter. 'This is our country too. Not only theirs. It's our birthright as much as it is theirs. We can't go on forever depending on other people, other societies, to rescue us. Those days are over. They are dead and gone. We must become our own masters, the makers of our own fate. That's what being independent means.' He waved his arms; his smock billowed. His eyes grew round and lustrous. 'We shouldn't just pack up our bundles and run off into exile. It's not right. It's not honourable.'

Ralph had laughed. 'It's not a question of right and honour. It's a question of survival.'

Dina recalled the appealing glance Aubrey had directed towards her.

She had said, 'Aubrey's right. This is our country, our place, whether we like it or not. We have no choice in the

58

matter. It is undignified to run off and become a refugee, to throw oneself on other people's mercy and beg for a visa '

How Aubrey's eyes had glowed with gratitude.

What Dina could have said was that she did not believe that the Plebiscite, the 'rewriting of the Constitution', would make the smallest difference to any of them; that it didn't matter whether there was or there wasn't a Constitution. She had never shared in the general intoxication roused by the Plebiscite. Whatever the result, it would not make their lives any more or less intolerable. It threatened nothing that was fundamentally new. They had, a long time ago, passed beyond the stage of mere corruption. What was called corruption had blossomed into a transcendence of its own. Banditry, cynicism and lies had been made a way of life; become, it could be said, an ideology.

'Behold your Paramount Chief,' the President had recently exulted at a rally of the faithful in Independence Park. An ecstatic chorus of affirmation had swelled through the warm night. As he spoke, he waved above his head the silver-pommelled cane he had adopted as his emblem of power and potency. The audience had danced, chanted, shrieked, sweated and swooned. Everything was already in place. Why then make such a fuss when there was nothing at stake? Why wrestle with shadows? Those queues outside the embassies infuriated her. The would-be refugees could all be condemned as accomplices. They had conspired to betray themselves. And now they were afraid. Their panic was, in its way, no less grotesque than the Plebiscite itself.

*

Consider Beatrice and Ralph. Who, in the end, had been bigger accomplices than they? Who, now, more frightened, more outraged, more ready to pack their bundles and run? For twenty years they had pandered and prospered. An assiduous courtier of the mighty, Ralph had insinuated himself into the President's confidence, mastered his lusts, and succeeded in establishing himself as his pet architect. It was Ralph, accommodating himself to the tastes of his client, who had been given the task of redesigning the interior of the Presidential Mansion.

'The vulgarity is stunning,' Beatrice had said, roaring with delight. 'You've never seen anything like it. Quite, quite stunning. Zebra skins, leopard skins, tiger skins, elephant tusks. Spears, shields, hideous masks. A swimming pool with artificial waves. Sunken baths. Saunas. Gold-plated taps. Claret-coloured silk on the walls. Boy! Did Ralphie let himself go on that one!'

Conscious, as Beatrice had said, of how and by whom their bread was buttered, they had adopted an indulgent attitude towards the excesses of their patrons. They had reaped the rewards that come from banditry, cynicism and lies.

Aubrey would often be angry with them. 'Why do you prostitute your talents on such wasteful enterprises?' he railed at Ralph. 'Do you know there are people dying of hunger in this country? You should be giving us low-cost housing, roads, schools. Those are the things you should be designing. That would be making a genuine contribution.'

Ralph did not lose his temper. He hardly ever did. Anyway, he was inured to Aubrey's lectures. 'Of course I agree with you, Aubrey. Who wouldn't? But, don't you think, as well as all those worthy projects you mentioned, a young nation needs some visible expressions of grandeur? Don't you think men need to be nourished on something more than bowls of plain, boiled rice?'

'I agree with you. I'm not a crass materialist. We must feed the spirit as well as the body.' Aubrey spoke with rising heat. 'But why all this imported marble and velvet? Who needs it? What does it actually achieve?'

Ralph had smiled, shaking his handsome, greying head. 'I do what my masters want me to do,' he said simply. 'As it happens, I don't think everything they do is as bad as you

60

suggest. Sure they can be a little excessive, a little too desirous of the shine and glitter – but so what? Anyhow, as their humble architect, mine's not to reason why. I do what they pay me to do. And what's wrong with that? It's not illegal, is it?'

Spreading his palms, Ralph grinned indulgently, changed the subject – and went on serving his masters and reaping the rewards. Beatrice, on her frequent trips abroad, had gradually amassed her sumptuous treasure of jewellery, jeering at Aubrey's 'idealism'. 'In this life, darlings,' she had said, 'you have to be realistic. You have to learn how to hunt with the hounds and run with the hare. You have to learn the art of flexibility. To bend with the wind like the willow. Like I do, darlings.'

Dina remembered how, hands on her waist, she had swayed and rotated her hips. Laughter had bubbled from her fleshy, scarlet lips. 'I know it's terribly vulgar, darlings. Sticks and stones may break my bones, but Aubrey's silly principles will never harm me.' Even more laughter had bubbled from those twin crescents of scarlet.

And suddenly, Beatrice, once so confident of her courtesan's influence in high places, was in a panic, carrying a gun in her handbag by day and burying it under her pillow by night. Suddenly, like so many of those who had been sharing in the loot, in the fruits of Independence (as the common phrase had it), she had realised that she was not immune; that the people's police and the people's soldiery did have in their possession sticks and stones that could break her bones. It was possible, almost casually, to become a victim of the banditry, the cynicism, the lies, in which they were all cocooned. Overnight she had grasped how unstable, how fragile a house of cards she had built. Like an ant crazed by the wanton destruction of its habitual routes of passage, she darted here and there, scurrying about in circles. It was ludicrous. It was pathetic. Dina was greatly disappointed in her friend – in this woman, so steeped in wordliness, who, from the very beginning of their acquaintance, had made it her business to teach her about life and its rich possibilities.

*

On the other hand, there were the people like Aubrey. All those letters, festooned with names, overflowing with indignation, showered like confetti on the editors of English and American newspapers, magazines and learned journals ... what did they expect this pitiable barrage to achieve? Those long, embittered wails of betrayal, of impassioned pleading, surfacing out of the ex-colonial darkness ... why should anyone bother to listen? That too was unbecoming and undignified.

What were the letter-writers hoping for? Did they envisage samite-clad legions, mystic, wonderful, dedicated to the salvation of suffering mankind, rushing to the rescue? What was he hoping for from his nicely balanced fusions of reason and emotion? Aubrey was not consistent. She was more consistent, clear-eyed and unsentimental than he was. If being independent meant, as he had said, being one's own master, it must also mean, by extension, being one's own victim. Self-sufficiency in all things! Theirs was not a unique case of decay. Nor, even, a particularly dramatic one. Social collapse, disorder, despair – these were the rule rather than the exception among those, like themselves, who had been cast out naked into the world and left to fend for themselves.

Vast tracts of the planet reeked of human anguish, of human decay. The surprising thing about the imminent abandonment of the Constitution – that lengthy charter so top-heavy with ringing preambles, so glutinously coated with abstract principles of right and justice and obligation, so ribboned with guarantees to minorities and special interests, so honeycombed with promises of life and liberty and happiness for all, so stiff with austere legalism, so sweetened with the codes of civility, that Constitution painstakingly fabricated and assembled over several weeks in panelled, chandeliered halls and flourished in triumph at the climax – the surprising thing was not that it was about to be unceremoniously tossed out of the window but that it had taken such a comparatively long time for that to happen.

Societies could not be created on sheets of parchment. They could not, even with the most golden of fountain pens, be signed into existence. Inevitably, men will succumb to their own reality. They will sink to the level of being where they feel most at ease with themselves. They would always act in conformity with their own natures and remake the world in their own image. The abandonment of the Constitution could be likened to a house settling into its foundations. That, more or less, was what was happening to them. They were falling prey to their own reality, settling into their foundations.

But what were the foundations into which they were settling? Were there, in fact, any foundations? It was possible that they would never stop sinking. There might be no bedrock beneath them. How far they might eventually be sucked down was anybody's guess. It was even possible that one day they might be entirely submerged. They might all be drowned. They could guarantee themselves nothing – not even bare survival. Seen in that light, the abandonment of the Constitution was mere child's play. The real horror was the endless sinking, the nightmarish reaching out for contract with the bedrock that would arrest their slow death by drowning – and not finding anything there.

Was it excessively uncharitable – 'defeatist' as Aubrey would have put it – to think like that? No doubt it was. But she could not help it. How passionately she hated this tropical sun, the never-ending succession of yellow afternoons, the foaming ugliness of the silted ocean. With what passion she hated the meanness, the ugliness, the brutishness of their lives. There was no sense to their existences. Nothing worthwhile had ever been created on this sterile patch of earth perched on the edge of a cruel continent; and nothing worthwhile ever would be. They had missed the boat. Not even divine intercession would make a difference in this vacuum imprisoned between ocean and jungle. Even the hurricanes which haunted the region avoided them, wreaking their vengeance on the islands to the north.

Only misery and death had been exhaled under this unrelenting sun – the primeval miseries of the small bands of wandering aborigines, worshipping fierce gods, living on roots and berries and small wild animals, periodically hunting each other's heads; the miseries of the second-rate conquistadors who had come looking for gold and finding none had gone mad with disappointment and blood-lust; the miseries of the slaves and their terrible revolts; the miseries of a fabricated statehood. The history of this patch of earth was written in blood. Pain was the only thing that had ever flourished on its red soil. Only in pain had they been self-sufficient. Submergence might come as a merciful release.

Yet how fervently Aubrey believed in the miracle of their transformation and redemption.

'We too,' he had once said to her, 'have our contribution to make to the history of mankind. All men have a part to play.'

How fervently he believed that. Or, rather, how fervently he insisted that he did. She sometimes wondered if he really did believe with all the warmth and conviction suggested by his vehemence. She sometimes wondered if there might not be a canker of doubt, a touch of desperation. But he would never let go of his faith. She herself, she knew, belonged to the realm of his faith. He had taken her into his life because he 'believed' in her. Belief gave his life its meaning. Without it, he would wither.

Yet, though she herself was so remote from his faith, so hostile, even, to the illusions he nourished, she realised that this place, however much it disgusted her, ran in her blood. Perhaps it ran in her blood even more than it did in his because she felt that, in some peculiar fashion, she had been hurt and deformed by it in ways that he had not. His agony was, to a certain extent, cerebral; hers was visceral. Its sterility and pain were part of her sterility and pain. Always, she would carry its hurt, its presence, with her. She would never escape its clutches.

Chapter Five

Through a break in the cloud cover, Alex Richer looked down on the wrinkled face of the Atlantic Ocean. The wake of an invisible ship was sliced like a lesion across its grey surface, emphasising the vastness of the vacancy below him. Sunlight flamed on the wings of the aircraft. The aircraft was full. Christmas was approaching and Cuyamese immigrants were returning home en masse for the occasion. At Heathrow, all had been confusion and turmoil. Bulging suitcases laced with rope, cardboard boxes of all shapes and sizes, had been manhandled on to the weighing scales. The December morning was chilly but the Cuyamese had succeeded in creating about themselves an enclave of almost tropical heat and humidity. 'Now, now,' the British Airways girl had appealed, 'it will be much easier for everyone if you form a queue. The aircraft isn't going to fly away and leave you behind.' Catching Alex's eye, she had released a confiding smile. Not being given to displays of tribal solidarity, he did not respond.

Boarding had been a no less perilous procedure than checking in. The Cuyamese had rushed at the aircraft much as if they were storming a barricade. He was pummelled, jostled, knocked about. One or two of his fellow passengers had nearly come to blows. The luggage racks were swiftly filled up; boxes and parcels were crammed in under the seats and overflowed into the aisles. The Air Cuyama stewardesses – engagingly quaint figures in sarong-style uniforms and flowered headscarves –were unable to impose their authority. After a few futile sallies and exhortations, they gave up, seeking asylum in the galleys where they huddled together helplessly. But now, three hours after take-off, with the Atlantic glinting far below, a semblance of order had been attained. Somehow lunch had been served and, in its aftermath, a dazed tranquillity pervaded the aircraft. The man next to him, occupying the window seat, was sleeping soundly, mouth agape. His arms embraced an extravagantly large, extravagantly shiny, music machine which was wedged on his lap: portability pushed to its limits. Alex studied the lustrous idol, festooned with knobs and dials, switches and gauges.

He called for a whisky. A button adorned with a photograph of the Cuyamese President was pinned on the breast of the sarong-clad stewardess who brought him the drink.

'Who's that?' Alex asked.

She glanced down at her breast. 'That is our President. A very great man.'

'What makes him a great man?'

'He is a liberator.'

'What has he liberated you from?'

'From colonialism. From the chains and shackles of imperialism.' Her brown, dreamy eyes met his. 'Because of him all Cuyamese can hold their heads high.'

'Ah . . .'

'He is a man with great pain in his heart for all the poor people of the world.' Her aspect changed to that of someone embarking on a fairy-tale. 'Once, you see, he himself was very poor and down-trodden. His mother was a washerwoman. His father was a mason, a bricklayer. As a boy, he had no proper clothes, no proper shoes even. Every day, in his bare feet, whatever the weather, he walked five miles to school. He has told us all about himself and about his struggle to get an education and make something of himself. You must read his autobiography. It is a most instructive and moving book. In the schools all Cuyamese children have to study it. He serves as an example to them.'

There was something oddly dignified in her manner which touched him. 'I'll buy a copy of the book. That's a promise.' He took a gulp of the whisky, relishing its warmth.

'A good friend of mine is Cuyamese,' he said. 'You may have heard of the family – the St Pierres.'

'St Pierre? I have heard of them but I do not know them. In the old days they had much money, much power. Now . . .' She shrugged. 'So, they're friends of yours?'

'No,' he said quickly, sensing her disapproval. 'Not the family as such. I knew a St Pierre at university. It's he who's my friend. I haven't seen him for many years. He owns a bookshop.'

'What's his name?'

'Aubrey.'

'Aubrey St Pierre.' The stewardess reflected. 'I do not know of him,' she said.

She left him. His neighbour, arms locked in embrace about his machine, snored lightly. The aircraft shuddered through a thunderous cloud formation.

'What may I ask is taking you to Cuyama, sir? Business? Pleasure?'

Alex turned towards the woman in missionary garb sitting across the aisle from him. Her pale blue eyes mooned at him out of a leathery face yellowed by long exposure to the tropical sun.

'Business,' he said. 'I'm a journalist.'

'A journalist.' She studied him with greater interest. 'You are going there to write about the People's Plebiscite?'

'That's the general idea.'

'You must be careful. They're very sensitive these days.'

'Aren't we all!'

'They do have a point, though,' she went on, unperturbed by his discouraging manner. 'Many journalists come, spend a day or two in the five-star luxury of the Park Hotel, chat over cocktails to one or two people who, more often than not, are hostile to the Government and what it's trying to

do. Then they go away and pass the most unbalanced judgments. For instance, that Aubrey St Pierre you mentioned –
he's a well-known critic of the Government. It's bad for
everybody when that happens.'

'What kind of unbalanced judgments do you have in
mind?'

Over the years he had become inured to such unsolicited
lectures – nearly always delivered by flourishing expatriates
who, on meeting him, became alarmed and appointed themselves spokesmen on behalf of the assorted barbarisms to
which they had successfully adapted themselves. They
seemed to regard it as their duty to point out to him that he
had set himself a hopeless task; that he was doomed to
misunderstand and misinterpret what he saw; that it was no
good importing metropolitan prejudices and trying to apply
them in an environment so radically different; that even
they, after years and years of residence ('And let me assure
you I was just as appalled to begin with as you are now . . .'),
were only just starting to appreciate the subtle, logical
necessities linking various outwardly distasteful phenomena
('It's a different way of looking at the world. You've got to
appreciate that . . .'). With what zest these types sang for
their supper!

'I'm sure,' came the reply, 'you know the kind of thing I
mean. The corruption and so on. Not that I'm denying there
is corruption. But, then, there's corruption everywhere, isn't
there?' The blue eyes wandered indulgently over his face.
'It's all too easy for outsiders like yourself to take a negative
approach. You seem only interested in the bad things. You
don't look at the positive achievements.'

'Which are?' Alex's eyes roamed the aisles.

'Take education, for example. More primary schools have
been built in the last ten years than in the previous hundred.
Nowadays, nearly every Cuyamese child gets some kind of
education. Or take health. There are now little clinics everywhere. Not very sophisticated, I admit – they can't afford

the equipment and the drugs – but better than having nothing at all, you'll surely agree. The Government has worked out a plan for training barefoot doctors, an idea the President got when he went to China last year.' The blue eyes warmed with emotion. 'I've given nearly half of my life to Cuyama. I remember very well what conditions were like when I first went out there. You can't begin to imagine what it was like then, how deeply neglected they were. Now they're getting back a little bit of their lost pride.' She regarded him sadly. 'Not that it's utopia. I'm not trying to suggest that. Have you heard of the Bush Folk?'

'As a matter of fact I have.' Alex showed greater interest.

'It's among them I live and do my work. In the Interior. Today, they're leaving the land, leaving the jungle which has supported and sheltered them for three hundred years. Many of the villages are half-deserted. Only the old people and children are left. The young ones cannot be persuaded to stay. They're tired of the old ways.' Her gaze rested on his companion cradling his lustrous machine. 'They want the things we have.'

'Progress,' Alex remarked. 'Everybody wants a share of the action. It's the same with the Eskimos, the Australian aborigines, everybody. Just as there's corruption everywhere, so everywhere there's progress, isn't there?'

Clasping together her yellow, freckled hands, she looked dolefully about her.

*

Alex closed his eyes. He seemed to hear Aubrey's voice – precise, erudite and sweetened with a tropical lilt.

'More than three-quarters of our land is covered by jungle. There are still one or two blanks to be filled in on the map of Cuyama. In the Interior, which most of us hardly know, are big rivers, waterfalls, cataracts, mountain ranges whose peaks have never been climbed. Some people believe that there one can find gold, diamonds, all kinds of precious stones. It's one of those fantasies which will never completely die. Those who have been there say it's extraordinarily beautiful. I have always dreamt of visiting the Interior. It fires my imagination.'

The bars of the electric fire glowed orange in the shabby, twilit room. Outside the English afternoon was damp and blue with mist. Aubrey sat in an armchair pulled up close to the fire, rubbing his hands, staring at the glowing bars. He had talked often about the Bush Folk – describing how those bands of fugitive slaves had formed themselves into tribes with hereditary chieftains; how they had abandoned Christianity, the religion of the white man, and evolved beliefs of their own, rooted in the traditions and practices of their African homeland. He described how each tribe had created a language of its own and how each had fabricated its own cycle of legends; how their women went about with bared breasts and did all the agricultural labour; how, away from the plantations, they had developed new skills, becoming expert hunters and boatmen. Aubrey talked and Alex listened.

'One of these days,' he had said, 'I would like to write something about the Bush Folk: a sort of cultural and political history. They have many lessons to teach us.'

The St Pierre family had provided Aubrey with another of his favourite themes. He talked at length about their history, telling how his ancestors had fled from Haiti after the slave uprising there in the early years of the nineteenth century and migrated to Cuyama where they had rebuilt their fortunes. He spoke of their activities with a mixture of pride and disparagement. To Alex, these tales of plantations cultivated with sugar, cotton, indigo and tobacco, of overseers and barracoons and beautiful Creole heiresses, were as alluring and as unreal as the stories in the Arabian Nights.

'My ambition,' Aubrey had said to him one day, 'is to devote myself to the welfare of my country and my people.

71

As a St Pierre, as a descendant of a long line of slave-owners, I feel that I have a special duty to do so.'

With what solemnity, what self-possession, he had uttered that avowal!

'You're quite priceless,' Alex remarked, grinning at him. Aubrey was, as usual, sitting on the armchair drawn close to the fire; he was untidily sprawled on the threadbare carpet, his arms clasped together under his head. 'Quite priceless,' he repeated.

'What are your ambitions?' Aubrey asked.

'I have none at all – certainly not in the sense you seem to mean.'

'Be serious.'

'I am being serious,' Alex replied. 'Who's waiting to be saved by the likes of me?'

'You can't possibly mean that,' Aubrey insisted. 'Everyone must have some larger reason to live, some cause to which they'd like to devote their lives. We can't only live for ourselves. Otherwise ...' Aubrey stared at the bars of the fire.

Alex raised himself up from the carpet. 'It's easy for you,' he said half-jokingly. 'You come from a long line of slave-owners. You have – or believe you have – the sins of your forefathers to expiate. You have a ready-made vocation, a country and a people waiting to be led from darkness to light. Conscience-stricken aristocrats like yourself have it made.'

'Are you accusing me of insincerity? Of hypocrisy?' Aubrey became grave.

'I'm not accusing you of anything. I'm merely pointing out the differences separating us.'

Aubrey continued to stare gravely at him. 'You'll discover in time what your vocation is,' he said. 'I feel sure of that.' He exuded a priestly solemnity.

Alex laughed. 'Good old Aub. You're incorrigible.'

Aubrey too had laughed and they had started to talk of other things.

Aubrey's earnestness had never ceased to astonish him. That earnestness, it eventually occurred to him, was underpinned by a peculiar deficiency of imagination; and by an intelligence which, looked at coldly, was not in any way remarkable. The essays Aubrey wrote were models of lucubratory competence. Yet, somehow, they were transfigured – touched by passion – when he read them out. His earnestness had a crystalline purity and perfection. No trace of cynicism or doubt blurred the clarity of that soul. At times, it was oppressive.

Aubrey seemed to have every aspect of his life mapped out. From that blueprint all intrusions of chance and misadventure had been excised. His was a passion grounded in literalness; in the inflexible faith that his sincerity could not go unanswered. The possibility that one day he might be knocked down and killed while crossing the street would never have presented itself to Aubrey. The future he outlined for himself was as complete, as formed, as the St Pierre past he was so fond of evoking when given the opportunity. It was almost as if it had already shaped itself in some sphere of being not immediately present to the crude senses. His mission, his wife, even his children – everything seemed to exist in embryonic wholeness.

'I do not care in the slightest what social class my wife comes from,' Aubrey had said. 'I do not have those kinds of prejudices. It's one of the many ways in which I differ from my family. They're obsessed by blood and background. Intelligence is all I ask. Intelligence combined with a willingness to share in my work. We'll be companions in a common endeavour, my wife and I. We'll be friends in the truest sense of the word.'

Aubrey had even enlarged on the system of education under which his children would be reared.

'And you, Alex,' he had asked, 'what will your wife be like?'

'Haven't given it a thought, Aub.'

73

'Come, come. You must have some notion of what you'd like in a wife. Some ideal ...'

'You and your ideals!' He frowned irritably. 'Still, if you insist on knowing, I'll tell you. I'd like a bird with a pretty face and big boobs. That's my ideal. Some simpering, over-scented, under-educated ...'

'Always the joker,' Aubrey said, regarding him indulgently.

Aubrey had not lacked girl friends. To the rooms they shared came a succession of comely young women whose acquaintance he had mysteriously made. Aubrey served them tea in his fine china cups and offered toast, biscuits and slices of cake. Punctiliously, he distributed paper napkins. Once or twice, Alex remembered, he had even provided wine – chilled, long-necked bottles of Rosé d'Anjou. Aubrey was quite the master of these sedate occasions, an accomplished conversationalist, the courteous gentleman removing coats from shoulders and restoring them at the hour of departure, the gallant escort who saw his visitors safely back to their rooms. Most of them seemed charmed by him. Aubrey, so far as he could tell, never strayed beyond the limits of propriety with his Antonias and Charlottes and Inges.

As always, he was not reluctant to expound his point of view. It was, he explained, his fixed intention to marry one of Cuyama's tropical blooms.

'A dusky maiden,' Alex smiled at him, 'with hibiscus in her hair?'

Aubrey sidestepped his levity. 'I've seen,' he said, 'too many marriages hastily conceived abroad end in disaster. I have no intention of falling into that trap. All of these girls you see coming here are admirable in their own environment. They're admirable because they belong to it. Remove them from it and there'll be disappointment and trouble. Like the Scarlet Ibis in captivity, they'll lose their colour, they'll fade away, they'll become sad shadows. I've seen that happen.'

In those hectic days of the 'sixties, Aubrey had stood out

with anachronistic splendour. He dressed as he talked – with pedantic elegance and precision. His shoes always shone; his trousers were always well-ironed; a silk handkerchief always adorned the breast pocket of his jacket. To behold Aubrey in his velvet dressing-gown, his feet encased in leather slippers, sipping his late evening mug of cocoa while warming himself at the electric fire ... this was to Alex – tangled hair falling to his shoulders, jeans modishly faded and patched, cheeks blued with stubble – a 'surreal' spectacle.

'You ought to loosen up,' Alex had urged one evening. He took an envelope from his pocket and made Aubrey sniff the contents. 'Do you know what it is?'

'Marijuana,' Aubrey said. 'It's not unknown in Cuyama. The Bush Folk use it as an intoxicant in certain of their religious rites.'

'And I use it in certain of mine. Will you share a joint with me?'

Aubrey considered the proposition. In the end, he agreed to give it a try.

'Well?' Alex asked, after they had each taken a few puffs from the joint he had rolled.

'I'm seeing colours,' Aubrey reported, eyes closed, head swaying rhythmically. 'I'm seeing all different kinds of colours.'

Alex laughed. However, this experiment in loosening up was never repeated. 'Once is quite enough,' Aubrey said. 'I wish to keep a clear head. You should too.'

'What for?'

Aubrey had sighed.

'I'm seeing colours ... I'm seeing all different kinds of colours ...' That remote avowal made Alex smile.

Yet, after the end of the first year, when they no longer shared rooms, they had begun to drift apart. Now and then, overcome by hunger late at night, he would go to Aubrey's room and raid his always well-stocked food cupboard. Aubrey, hands buried in the pockets of his velvet dressing-

75

gown, was as generous with his food, as welcoming, as ever. But their conversation was stilted and desultory. It was as though they had nothing left to talk about; as though they had exhausted each other's repertoire. Sometimes, Aubrey would drop in on him, but the crowd that was usually assembled there did not appear to appeal to him and he would soon leave. In their final year, when they moved into digs in town, the distance between them had increased even further. Alex, belatedly fired by the desire to get a good degree, worked hard and wretchedly, virtually incarcerating himself in the stacks of the library; a penitence intermittently relieved by spasms of debauchery. Long intervals passed by without him catching a glimpse of Aubrey. When it was all over he had fled without even bothering to say goodbye. He had flung his few clothes and some books into a canvas hold-all, jumped on a bus heading in the direction of the railway station – and was gone. He had all but forgotten about Aubrey when a magazine, for which he had written a series of articles, forwarded to him a letter embellished with the gaudy stamps of the Republic of Cuyama.

'During all these long years (went the letter) I have never ceased to think of you and to wonder where life has taken you. I was a little hurt that you should run off without a word. Not even a forwarding address ... Imagine, therefore, my unspeakable delight when, on receiving this magazine (which, incidentally, I read avidly), I should see your name so prominently displayed on its cover. At first, I did not dare believe that it might be you. Possibly, I thought, this is quite another Alexander Richer. But the biographical details provided dispelled all doubt. My dear Alex – how are you? Fraternal greetings from your Cuyamese comrade! You have, I see, found your vocation. Your skill and your talent shine through in every line you write. Those Tanzanian articles of yours are no mere passing pieces of journalism. I salute you.

'I myself have nothing of great moment to report. Life in

Cuyama is an endless challenge. But I never allow myself to lose heart. Underdevelopment, as I'm sure you would agree, is not only an economic phenomenon. It has a spiritual dimension as well; as much a state of mind as a state of exploitation. The underdeveloped economy is based on the underdeveloped personality. We will only begin to make progress when that personality starts to transform itself.

'Latterly, I've become a tradesman of sorts. Three months ago I opened a bookshop – a bookshop, dare I say, dedicated to propagating the highest standards in literature. I try to stock only the best on my shelves. Commercial success is not my primary aim, though, of course, I would like to see the enterprise break even. It pleases me to think that through it I am making a modest contribution to the spiritual uplift of the Cuyamese people.

'Whenever I can, I myself put pen to paper – articles on topics of local interest, literary criticism and, now and again, a short story. I do not, alas, have your talent. Nevertheless, I persevere. Effort, I believe, is its own reward. Without effort, there is nothing. Constant labour, as Balzac has said, is the law of art as well as the law of life. Well, my dear Alex, I am a constant if not a talented labourer!

'I still recall with pleasure the talks we used to have, me sitting on the armchair by the electric fire, you sprawled on the floor. Do you remember? Or have you completely forgotten? If this letter ever does reach you and you have the time and inclination, do drop me a line. Old friends like us should not sail past each other like ships in the night.'

A card was enclosed. 'The Aurora Bookshop. Books To Feed The Mind And Gladden The Soul.'

Alex filed away the letter and the card.

He never replied.

About a year later he received another, forwarded by the same magazine.

'I have no idea if you received the previous letter I wrote to you. Nor do I have any idea if this one will reach you.

Still, I consider it both a duty and a pleasure to make the attempt to inform you that soon I shall be shedding my bachelor status. It has taken me a long time to find the partner I've always dreamt about. Dina – that is the name of my wife to be – is everything I could have wished for . . . and more. She is the daughter of a schoolteacher and has a degree in English Literature from the University of Cuyama. She is an intelligent and serious-minded girl. Ours, to my mother's regret, will be a civil marriage because Dina is Presbyterian. My family is fervently Catholic. Dina has never travelled abroad, a state of affairs that will be rectified on our honeymoon. I plan to under-take a grand tour of sorts so that she can see at first hand some of the marvels she has only read about or heard about or seen in photographs. We will be spending a little time in London which is our first stop. It goes without saying that nothing would give me greater delight than to see you again, Alex.

'Dina and I met in somewhat unusual circumstances. She was one of several applicants for the post of assistant in my bookshop which I'd advertised in the newspaper. (If you did not receive my previous letter, you won't know what I'm talking about: briefly, about a year ago, I opened a bookshop.) She was the only one of the applicants properly qualified for the job. Indeed, with her degree in English Literature, she was far too well qualified! Who would have guessed that the woman I had begun to despair of ever finding would enter my life in so curious and improbable a fashion? Who would have guessed that she would arise out of the Situations Vacant columns? Do, I beg you, make contact if this letter reaches you. Meeting you would com-plete my happiness.'

Enclosed was an invitation to the wedding. It was an elaborate production, adorned with scalloped edges and embossed gold lettering. 'Do excuse the unbecoming osten-tation,' Aubrey had scribbled on the bottom. 'My own taste suggested a simpler and more austere design. My mother, regrettably, would have it no other way but this.'

Stephanie St Pierre, widow of the late Charles Aubyn St Pierre, was pleased to announce to Mr Alexander Richer the forthcoming marriage of her son, Aubrey Eugene St Pierre, to Dina Marie Mallingham, daughter of Roy Stephen Mallingham and Rose Deborah Mallingham of Greenfield Gardens, Charlestown. Stephanie St Pierre cordially requested the pleasure of Mr Alexander Richer's company at the luncheon reception to be held in the Ball Room of the Park Hotel, Independence Park South, Charlestown.

Alex filed away the letter and the invitation.

He never replied.

Alex had had no further reminders of Aubrey's existence – until he had seen the letter in *The Times*.

'Sir, it is with a sense of deep shame and outrage that we, the undersigned, citizens from all walks of life, feel impelled to draw your readers' attention to the threatened abuse of fundamental human and political rights which, under the smokescreen of constitutional reform, is about to take place . . .' etc, etc.

He remembered how he had laughed when, out of the blue, the idea had presented itself to him. Capriciously, while re-reading the letter over breakfast, he had been pricked by a desire to see Aubrey.

Summoning the stewardess, Alexander Richer called for another whisky.

*

A day or two before Alex's arrival, Aubrey had presented Dina with the series of articles he had written on Tanzania.

'I thought it would be nice for you to have some idea of his work,' he said.

Installing herself in the sun-bleached deck chair, she had sat out in the garden, in the shade of the orange-tree, and read them. Alex's writing was taut and elegant; livened by eccentric personal touches and flourishes: so different from Aubrey's laboured productions, starched with statistics, dulled by the anaesthetic modes of expression he had picked up from the political and sociological treatises to which he was addicted. While he struggled for 'objectivity' – one of his favourite words – Alex, it struck her, was unabashedly subjective. She was surprised that an approach so alien in style and substance from his own should have won his admiration.

'What Alex has to say about the *ujamaa* programme is sensible and balanced,' Aubrey observed.

Balanced. Sensible. These Aubreyisms jarred.

'I'm surprised his work appeals to you so much,' she ventured.

'Why?' Aubrey wrinkled his brows at her.

'I would have thought he would be a little too subjective for your tastes.'

'I take your point. If Alex has a fault it is just that. He does stray towards self-indulgence.' Aubrey, playing with his beard, became thoughtful. 'Alex,' he said, 'was a true child of the 'sixties. There was hardly a fad that passed him by. He grew his hair long, smoked hashish and marijuana, tripped out – as the phrase has it – on LSD, listened to rock music day and night. Alex did it all.'

'What about you?' Dina asked. 'Weren't you ever tempted by any of that?' There was mischief in the question.

'Me?' Aubrey, not noticing the mischief, displayed some astonishment at the suggestion. 'I didn't see the point of it at all. Not that I was – or am – against people enjoying themselves. The desire for pleasure is perfectly natural ...'

Dina laughed.

'What are you laughing at?'

'Nothing.'

'Mind you,' he said, 'I did try marijuana once.'

'You did?'

'Largely to satisfy Alex.'

'Did you like it?'

Aubrey shrugged.

'It had no effect on you?' Was there nothing, she wondered, with power sufficient to alter, even temporarily, the balance of the well-ordered mind confronting her? Was there nothing that could divert it into more erratic by-ways? She thought of herself and Beatrice eating the hashish-laced fudge Beatrice had concocted one idle afternoon and succumbing to fits of giggles. She had never told Aubrey about that escapade – after which she had been violently sick in Beatrice's bathroom. She looked away from him, out to the empty street and the blackened, graffiti-defaced walls of the church: they were talking in the bookshop, during those dead hours of mid-afternoon when no one ever ventured near the place; when, without harm to its commercial prospects, it could have shut its doors against an unresponsive world. Her mood deteriorated.

'This Alex of yours,' she said, 'he specialises in our sort, does he?'

'How do you mean, "our sort"?' He had never found it easy to keep track of her abrupt alterations of mood. In an instant, she could move from laughter to ferocity, from ferocity to contrition, from contrition to irony, from irony to something akin to tenderness, from tenderness to indifference. Her emotions, ceaselessly transformed, ceaselessly rearranging themselves, were kaleidoscopic in their mutability. 'How do you mean, "our sort"?' he repeated.

'You know – the Third World. Sympathy for the darker races of mankind in their struggle against oppression.'

The sleeves of his smock billowed as his arms swept upwards. 'You've just said how much you liked his work.'

'The articles you showed me were excellent.'

'Then why did you say what you just said?'

'I don't know.' She looked at him sombrely. 'Forget it. I was just being stupid.'

'We need all the help we can get,' he said, electing to

revert to the concrete. 'It's a great coup for us to have him coming out here.'

'I believe you. I'm sure he'll do a wonderful job.' She frowned, staring out at the bright afternoon, blinking into the hard glare.

'I wish you would tell me what's wrong, what's troubling you.'

She began to cry. It was not often that she showed him her tears. Even on their honeymoon, sitting at the window, looking down at the moonlit lake, she had hidden them from him. Her tears were part of her privacy. They belonged to that part of herself about which he knew so little – nothing at all really.

He reached out an arm to her.

Involuntarily, she recoiled.

Stopping dead, he did not touch her. For a moment or two he let the arm remain extended in its thwarted gesture; then let it drop slowly to his side.

*

The aircraft, tilting, revealed on one side, beyond a sun-flamed wing, an unclouded expanse of blue, of infinite space; while on the other there was exposed to view an expanse of sedimented ocean infiltrated by tongues of aquamarine washing a blurred, low-lying wisp of coastline which faded away over the edge of the horizon. It was a bleak and sullen scene; stark, elemental and amphibious in character: a primeval oozing together of earth and water and sky. Roused from torpor, excited Cuyamese pressed their faces against the windows, gesticulating and babbling at each other. A broad estuary appeared, a gash sliced through the melting land, bleeding its brown blood into the ocean. A series of long, boat-shaped islands lay marooned in it. They were clothed in dense, unbroken green – images of isolation and abandonment unmarked by the hands of man. Soon, however, river and ocean were lost to sight and there was only the jungle exhaling breaths of cloudy vapour. The cruciform shadow of the aircraft slithered across the sunlit immensity of tree-tops. The man beside him, still embracing his extravagantly large, extravagantly shiny, music machine, stared down with vacant intensity at the wilderness which, here and there, was dissected by the black, winding ribbons of smaller streams; the missionary dozed. They dropped ever closer to the desolation, broken in the far distance by a range of hills, very blue, above whose ridges the air steamed and trembled in a white haze. Again Alex cursed the dismal whim that had brought him to so blighted a corner of the planet. The jungle thinned. He saw clearings of red earth, the rotting boles of felled trees tossed about like matchsticks.

They were informed that, within a minute or two, they would be landing at Cuyama International Airport.

*

Long before the aircraft had come to a standstill, Cuyamese were crowding the aisles, groping and fumbling in the overhead luggage racks and under the seats, stumbling and falling over each other. His companion, clutching his lustrous idol, clambered over him and vanished into the mêlée. Alex remained where he was, gazing out at the uninviting prospect. A grey-green gloom of forest rose like a wall on the far perimeter. Birds of prey soared and circled in the pearly haze. Heat waves shimmered on the scalding tarmac, creating watery mirages reflecting the sky and the wheeling birds. A gush of overheated, humid air swirled through the open doors of the aircraft, bringing with it intimations of tepid earth and decay.

He was one of the last to disembark, moving slowly through the daze of heat and light towards the squat, grey shed of a building that served as the terminal. From tall poles rising out of a narrow strip of lawn running parallel to its dour façade, the green, red and yellow flag of the Republic hung lifeless in the stationary noon. Clumps of hibiscus, bougainvillaea and poinsettia glowed brightly but without gaiety. Soldiers attired in combat fatigues, rifles aslant on their shoulders, lurked in the shade of the eaves.

A triumphal arch proclaimed in gold lettering: Welcome To The Republic Of Cuyama. One People. One Struggle. One Redeemer.

The Immigration Officer, encased in stiff khaki, looked from the photograph in the passport to his face. Having, after a protracted scrutiny, satisfied himself that the former was indeed an accurate rendering of the latter, he began leafing through the pages of the passport, examining every stamp recorded there. Alex adopted the manner that had become usual with him in such circumstances, hunching himself into a stance of propitiatory calm and fortitude. The missionary smiled with blue-eyed sympathy at him, a smile transferred with benevolent neutrality to the Immigration Officer whose coal-complexioned, bony countenance happened, at that moment, to turn in her direction. More soldiers in combat fatigues patrolled the cavernous hall beyond, rifles aslant on shoulders.

He turned his attention to the portrait of the President of the Republic affixed to the partition behind the officer's desk. He studied the unsmiling face from which every suggestion of a blemish had been eradicated by the cunning art of the developer. The fleshy cheeks were as smooth and as silky as chocolate; the lips were full and shapely and sensual; the line of the jaw was firm; the almond-shaped eyes, slightly protuberant and hooded by drooping lids, exuded a hibernatory potency of will. He sensed the parody of dictatorship that had descended – or was about to formally descend – on Cuyama.

The washerwoman's son who had walked barefoot to school every day ... who, as a child, had never had enough to eat ... who had triumphed over insult and humiliation ... who, with painstaking effort, had taught himself to read and write ... The hagiography was simplicity itself. It was so easy to heap scorn on it. But it may have been like that. All he may have done was condense his individual experience into an abstracted essence, transforming himself into a metaphor with which the mass of his countrymen could commune: a metaphor at once immediately recognisable and transcendent – a magical folk-tale ending in this radiance of physical perfection and unblemished prowess. The deepest dreams of the downtrodden had little to do with what was called development. Their degradation, Alex had divined, spawned dreams of another order altogether. The face he looked at spoke not of bridges and roads and hospitals and clean drinking water. It evoked all the phantasmagoria of miraculous transformation and redemption, of power untrammelled, unaccountable and mystical, of oppressors scattered like dust in the wind. The face he looked at mirrored a yearning beyond the reach of mere words and mere political programmes. They were all, in a manner of speaking, washerwomen's sons and daughters; they had all walked barefoot on the hard, red earth; they had never, any of them, had enough to eat and drink; they had, without exception, been insulted and humiliated almost beyond endurance.

One Man. One People. One Struggle.

In the end, the stamp fell. The Republic of Cuyama gave him permission to stay on its territory for one week.

Chapter Six

Aubrey was instantly recognisable among the milling crowd. His immaculateness, his precision of form, was not disguised by the smock and baggy trousers. They fell into each other's arms, embracing, laughing. Aubrey had visibly aged. There was a touch of grey on his sideboards. There was, too, something else: a suggestion of fatigue in the depths of the eyes. They had shed a portion of their optimistic assurance.

'You've become older and wiser,' Alex joked. 'I can see that life has revealed one or two of its more debilitating mysteries to you.'

Aubrey did not respond to the challenge.

Aubrey picked up the suitcase and led him out into the brilliant afternoon. Urchins rushed up to him, offering their services. He fended them off gently. Alex breathed in the scorched odours of warm earth. Insects flashed and buzzed. His shadow was a black, dwarfish flame. He stared at the distant wall of jungle.

They arrived at the Morris Minor.

'Only the big boys are allowed new cars,' Aubrey said. 'The hoi polloi like myself must catch as catch can. The hunt for spare parts has become the national pastime.'

Alex manoeuvred himself into the cramped, scalding interior of the car. Aubrey, in his billowy smock, baggy trousers and sockless sandals, was to him no less insubstantial, no less immaterial, than the mocking pools of liquescence conjured up by the heat. Ahead of them, the narrow ribbon of asphalt uncoiled between walls of scrubby jungle. Alex, eyes narrowed against the glare, listened to Aubrey's lamentations.

'I could never get over the way you disappeared just like that. Once I went round to your room and cross-questioned your landlady. I simply didn't know what to think.'

'It wasn't very thoughtful of me, was it?'

Out of the tangled, vine-encrusted profusion rose palm trees of many varieties, their foliage glistening in the sunlight. Clumps of orange-coloured lilies flared up among colonies of fern and drooping grasses. Far away, a stain against the white sky, was a serration of hills. There was little other traffic; yet, Aubrey drove slowly.

A pyre of smouldering charcoal sent up a grey fog of smoke in a clearing scattered with the stumps of felled trees. At the jungle edge of the clearing was a low hut thatched with palm leaves. Within its shade sat a man in ragged clothing, wearing knee-high boots, a cutlass resting on his knees. Nearby, a white bird perched on a blackened stump.

'At the time,' Alex said, 'it seemed the only thing to do. After three years, I just wanted to clear out, to put the maximum distance between myself and that place. To cut and run.' He gazed at the serrated hills.

'Why didn't you leave a forwarding address?' After all that time, the reproach was tired. It lacked energy and conviction: the period of mourning was long over.

'I didn't have a forwarding address to leave,' Alex said. 'I simply stuffed what clothes I had into my canvas bag, took a bus to the station and boarded the next train to Paddington. I had no idea where I would go or what I would do when I got there. For weeks I lived like a tramp, dossing down wherever I could.'

A flock of parrots swooped across the road and vanished over the tree-tops.

'I remember that canvas bag of yours very well,' Aubrey said. Decelerating, he gingerly eased the car across a pothole. 'Did you ever get any of those letters I wrote to you?'

'No.' He disliked the petty lie. But to admit that he had

received them would have led him into regions of explanation where he had no desire to venture.

'I even sent you an invitation to my wedding.'

'Your wedding!' Alex did his best to simulate surprise. 'Tell me all.'

Aubrey told him what he could. 'And you?' he asked. 'What about you?'

'Matrimony didn't agree with me.'

A lorry, its open tray piled with bricks, planks of wood and sheets of corrugated iron, was approaching. It had arrogated to itself the middle of the narrow road. Aubrey took evasive action, angling off on to the gravelled verge and coming to a halt. The lorry, belching black smoke, roared and rattled past them. They resumed their cautious progress.

'My little mésalliance,' Alex went on, 'lasted for about six weeks – give or take a day or two.' The skin round his eyes puckered.

'I'm sorry.' Aubrey rested a sad, brown regard upon him.

'Nothing to be sorry about. Divorce was like a mercy killing, like shooting a wounded horse. The mistake lay in getting hitched, not in dissolving a union sanctified by man but certainly not blessed by God. He just wasn't around that day. It was one of those quick Registry Office jobs.'

'So was mine,' Aubrey remarked, smiling at him.

'And is it blessed by God?'

Aubrey seemed not to hear the question.

The hills were now more defined. Alex could pick out the shaded pools of the valleys separated by sunlit ridges. At intervals, there rose spirals of wavering smoke – bush fires. He could see more extensive, already burnt-out patches scarring the slopes. Circling vultures floated high in the white sky.

A concrete bridge with crumbling parapets crossed a ravine whose sombre waters vanished in the green gloom amid a tangle of roots, fern and mossy outcrops of rock.

Referendum slogans were daubed along the sides of the parapet.

One Nation. One Party. One Leader.

Death To The Traitors.

'Who are the traitors?' Alex asked. 'People like yourself?'

'People like myself. Anybody who opposes their plans.'

'Do you suppose they mean what they say?'

Aubrey heaved his shoulders.

'You aren't ever afraid of what might happen to you one of these days?'

'What happens to me is of no consequence.'

The windscreen of an approaching car glinted in the distance.

Aubrey, preparing for evasive action, glanced at him. 'If you were me, would you be afraid? Would you let yourself be intimidated by your personal fears?'

'I don't know,' Alex replied. 'I'm not sure what my beliefs are – or even if I have any.'

'Come ... come ...' The oncoming car was safely negotiated.

'I'm a dilettante. A moral butterfly. A month here, two weeks there, a few days somewhere else. I'm not a serious person.' He stared at the spirals of smoke coiling up from the flanks of the hills.

Aubrey wagged his head at him. For a while, they drove in silence.

'Is your lady everything you hoped she would be? I remember ...' But some instinct made Alex check his words; choked off the memories he was on the verge of resurrecting.

Aubrey hunched himself lower over the steering wheel, biting his lips. He did not answer straight away. 'Dina,' he said at last, 'is a complex person. In a place like this (he waved at the wilderness), in a society so limited in its choices, so restricted in the range of expression it permits ... in such a place the intelligence does not have a great deal to

feed on. It often gets smothered by the challenging emptiness and sameness. It seems to collapse in on itself. To
undergo a kind of implosion – if you know what I mean.'

Silence again fell. The jungle was abating, giving way to
stretches of more open country. Here and there, set back
from the road, were little wooden houses on stilts and
palm-thatched mud huts. A ragged girl, with a bronzed,
aboriginal face, a baby propped on her hip, stopped to watch
them go by. Alex waved at her, but she did not respond. She
stood there, amidst the roadside grasses, impassive, the
baby clamped on her hip; a dumb, primal emanation.

'I've talked to Dina about you often,' Aubrey said. He
dried his damp forehead with the sleeve of his smock.

Alex looked at him, but offered no comment.

'She was tremendously impressed by your Tanzanian articles.'

Alex brushed aside the compliment.

There was more traffic on the road now and Aubrey drove
with even greater caution. They dodged an unsteady bicy-
clist transporting a bundle of grass on his handlebars.

'In those talks we used to have, did I ever mention a man
called Boniface?' Aubrey asked.

'I can't remember.' Alex gazed out at the disordered
desolation. 'Who's he?'

'He was one of the great leaders of the Bush Folk. Back in
the eighteenth century he vowed he would drive the whites
out of Cuyama and he nearly succeeded. I'm sure I must
have mentioned him to you.'

Alex took himself back to the room they had once shared.
The romance, however, had been sucked out of Aubrey's
stories. The horrors depicted by those tales now lay too close
to hand, irradiating the tepid breezes swirling through the
open windows of the car. 'You may have done,' he said.

'Boniface is now our National Hero,' Aubrey went on.
'Just as we have a National Flower and a National Bird and a
National Tree so we have also provided ourselves with a

National Hero.' Aubrey laughed. 'I thought that might amuse you. Boniface has his monument in Republic Square – formerly Victoria Square. The old statue of the Queen was removed and he was installed in her place.' He lifted a hand off the steering wheel, flicking a supple wrist. 'Now there's something you should take a look at. Some years ago the President decided that it was politically improper to have relics of our former rulers disfiguring the squares and public places of Charlestown. As a result, virtually every monument dating from the colonial period has been removed and dumped in an obscure corner of the Botanical Gardens. They make a bizarre spectacle.'

'Did you ever try to write that book about the Bush Folk?' Alex asked.

'No. Somehow, I never seemed to find the time.' The dark eyes dimmed with melancholy.

They were entering sugar-cane country. The fields rolled away across the undulating plain towards the hills; a sea of emerald green tufted with feathery arrowheads gleaming like silk in the brilliant light. In the distance, the chimneys of a refinery pierced the green tide. A near continuous ribbon of settlement now bordered the road on one side. Alex looked at the wooden houses, raised on pillars, with flights of stairs leading to small verandas where, on this Sunday afternoon, families were congregated. Girls in bright dresses leaned on veranda rails, staring out across the canefields, or paraded arm in arm along the roadside. Hammocks, slung in the pillared space beneath the houses, swayed slowly. Tattered, faded pennants – red, white, green, yellow – drooped from bamboo poles screened behind rough hedges of hibiscus. Mongrels rushed out of unkempt yards, chasing the car, snapping and snarling at the wheels. Out of the mud slime of the ditch bordering the road fetid odours pushed up through the reeds.

'Hindustani area,' Aubrey remarked parenthetically. 'Therefore, a case study in neglect. One strand of the glorious cultural tapestry of which we Cuyamese boast so much.'

Alex took in the squalor and decay; the dirt and ugliness of this ribbon of settlement cramped between fields of sugar-cane and scrubland edged with forest. He stared at the ragged prayer flags on their bamboo poles, at the orange and red hibiscus flowers showing in the hedges, at the unkempt children exploring the margins of the water-channels, at the pubescent girls in their bright dresses, sun-darkened faces gazing out over the rustling fields of cane. Only the dogs baring their teeth in mindless fury had mastered the art of responding to this celebration of human futility clamped down between fields and forest.

A van with loudspeakers attached to its roof emitted a screech of Bombay film music. In a voice hoarse with exertion, the driver shrieked the glories of forthcoming Indian films. In the shade of a mango tree a group of men squatted, playing cards and drinking rum. A temple, sheltered in a grove of palms, appeared on the left. Its white-washed walls and crude dome were decorated with gaudy representations of the Hindu divinities. Nearby, a naked child, its brown skin glistening in the sunlight, was dousing himself at a wayside standpipe. As they passed, he directed a spray of rainbow-tinted water at the sides of the car. Turning away, Alex looked at the burning hills.

The ribbon of settlement thinned and died away. They were in open, marshy country, dotted with dessicated mud-flats framed by clumps of tall, reddish-green grass. A solitary buffalo raised its head, acknowledging their passage. Herons stood still in the dark desolation. They joined the main Charlestown highway. The hills were now on their right and the sun fell full on their faces. Small plots of cultivation and little ramshackle houses and huts were scattered over the plain. Distant figures, dwarfed by the sky and the hills, hoed and raked and weeded. But, mostly, the land lay waste, a wilderness of windswept grasses and reeds, of spindly trees and stony earth dotted with the fissured beds of dried-up ponds. A lorry, bumping over a rutted track, raised a rolling mist of red dust. Here and there coconut palms reared enigmatically out of the waste, their trunks arched like the necks of browsing prehistoric monsters. Pedestrians paused and waved at them from the verges, hoping for a ride into town. But Aubrey did not stop. He was talking about the Plebiscite, expounding in greater detail the substance of the letter he had had published in *The Times*, accompanying the exposition with a prodigal variety of gestures. The sleeve of his smock ballooned and snapped with small, staccato explosions of emphasis.

Alex listened languidly, head tilted back against the frame of the window, eyes half-closed, face exposed to the raw blast of sun and whipping wind. Aubrey's words came to him in gusty snatches. The vehement passions they conveyed seemed to reach him after travelling a great distance, arriving at their destination ragged and incomplete: as remote, as unreal, as the roar of the ocean heard in a seashell. A rattling bridge, its silver-painted superstructure disfigured with slogans, took them across a brown, slow-flowing stream trellised and knitted with mangrove. On the muddy bank a funeral pyre was ablaze, causing the air to shimmer like a sheet of melting glass. A crowd of mourners contemplated the spectacle, watching the smoke, the shimmering air, the reflection of the flames in the water.

Alex struggled to find speech. 'I take it,' he managed to say as the highway curved out of sight of the river and the blazing pyre, 'there's no question of the President not having his way, that the deed's as good as done.'

Aubrey indicated his assent. 'But that doesn't mean we must give up. The struggle must continue.' He turned towards him. 'That is why it's so important for us to have someone like you come out here.'

Alex avoided his scrutiny. Just as all those years ago he had recoiled from the tyranny of Aubrey's sincerity, so now he found himself recoiling from this new tyranny of expectation. The urge to run away from him reasserted itself with all its old vigour. He recalled the time he had literally done so: when Aubrey had hailed him on the High Street and he had fled into a shop which specialised in herbal preparations. Now, for no clear reason, he thought of the girl – that Dina with her degree in English Literature and her imploded intelligence – whom Aubrey had plucked out of the hot Cuyama air and had made his bride. Had she been ground to dust by the tyranny of his uncomprehending affection? Did she too occasionally yearn to run away from him? But where could one run to in a place like Cuyama?

'Your wife ...' he heard himself saying.

Aubrey looked at him.

Alex relapsed into silence.

Aubrey continued his vehement discourse.

The landscape was changing, shedding its rural character, acquiring a semi-urban aspect. They passed a rum distillery, rows of warehouses, small workshops. At a busy junction a beggar with matted hair lurched out into the traffic, thrust his hand into the car and demanded money. Aubrey ignored him. The man banged a fist on the roof as they crept forward. Beyond the junction, the road climbed into the hills. Groups of blacks lounged aimlessly in the red, roadside dust. Above them, on slopes dissected by winding tracks, a dense slum colony had established itself. Boys danced out into the road, flourishing sun-withered fruit and vegetables. The big, scalloped leaves of breadfruit trees shone in the sunlight.

Climbing, the road threaded itself through sliced walls of rock. Then, on the right, the wall broke to reveal the valleys of the Coastal Range sweeping away eastward. Scattered groves of bamboo imparted a deceptive vernal freshness to the forested slopes. A coiling plume of smoke rose from a distant ridge. In the depths below, a trickle of a stream meandered among rocks and sand-spits. The road continued its serpentine ascent. On the left too the wall of rock broke.

Alex was startled by the sight of the sea, patterned with cloud-shadows. Charlestown sprawled out from the foot of the hills, its jumbled roofs spreading to the edge of the water. Aubrey indicated various landmarks – the spire of the Roman Catholic cathedral, the green dome of the Assembly Building, the oval expanse of Independence Park which, at that height, was visible in its entirety. He pointed out the curving façade of the Park Hotel on the far side of the park.

'I've booked you in there,' he said. He hesitated. 'It was there Dina and I had our wedding reception.'

The road began to descend, tracing out a series of loops and hairpin bends.

They emerged on the northern perimeter of the park. Aubrey drew Alex's attention to the turrets of the Presidential Mansion, the tranquil glades of the Botanical Gardens, the once-handsome row of wood-built colonial mansions, adorned with tiled roofs and gables, which lined the park's western fringe. Several of these had been converted into Government offices. Others, it seemed, were being allowed to decay. Alex stared into overgrown gardens and caught glimpses of verandas almost overwhelmed by the leafage of unpruned trees and shrubs.

Beeping his horn, Aubrey turned off into the quiet street with the church on the corner, the church whose electric cross glowed blue by night, and came to a halt outside a tall green gate near which a signboard, obscured in part by the branches of an oleander, projected like a stiffened flag over the pavement.

'The Aurora Bookshop. Books To Feed The Mind And Gladden The Soul.'

Chapter Seven

Dina, face half-hidden by a pair of dark glasses, wearing a simple dress of pink cotton that left her arms bare, rose out of the wrought-iron chair as Aubrey preceded him out on to the back veranda.

'Here he is! Here he is!' Aubrey moved before him like a herald.

A slender arm, pale brown on its underside, striped by a network of bluish veins, showing at the shoulders a vaccination scar, was extended towards him.

She smiled. 'Welcome.'

The hand he briefly held in his own was limp and warm.

'While you're in Cuyama,' Aubrey said, 'you must treat this place as your own, come and go as you please. No standing on formality. Mia casa ès sua casa.' He bustled about, arranging chairs.

'Maybe you'd like to have a wash,' she said.

'Go on,' Aubrey urged. 'It will do you good to have a wash. While you're doing that I'll mix the famous St Pierre rum punch for you. The recipe's a family secret, handed down through the generations from father to son – to be divulged only on pain of instant disinheritance.' He laughed.

She led him into the house and up the stairs to a tiny, tiled cubicle of a bathroom which, he could tell at a glance, had been made ready for his intrusion. Virtually all traces of its usual occupants had been removed. Only a shower-cap hanging from a nail testified to the ablutions she performed in that cell. The finicky self-effacement amused him. She tried the tap. Brownish water trickled.

'You're lucky,' she said. 'The water's actually running. Don't be put off by the colour.'

'Doesn't it usually run?'

'The supply is extremely erratic. There are days when it doesn't run at all. Hence the buckets.' Blinking, she indicated a row of buckets filled with water. 'I'm afraid there isn't any hot water.' She heaved her shoulders. 'But then . . . who needs it? I'm sorry it's so primitive.'

Her small laugh bounced and echoed off the walls. She ran her eyes over the fresh towels, the virginal cake of soap – and left him.

*

When, some fifteen or twenty minutes later, he returned to the veranda, the rum punch had been mixed. The orange-coloured liquid was contained in a large bowl of clear glass round the rim of which glass cups were suspended from glass hooks. Aubrey stirred the concoction with a glass ladle (the ensemble had been a wedding present from his mother) and doled out the measures.

'Taste!'

Alex tasted. 'Ambrosial,' he murmured, licking his sugared lips, settling himself more deeply into his chair, staring out at the sun-dappled square of garden, at the vine foaming over the fence. Everything seemed more dreamlike than ever – Aubrey, the woman he called his wife, himself, the hot square of garden: shadows whose actions and words he did not fully understand.

Aubrey exhibited his daughter. The child's dark, rounded eyes ruminated on him for a while. Turning away, she buried her face between her father's knees. Aubrey, chiding her for her shyness, cradled her head. The resemblance of father and daughter was uncanny. Alex could detect few traces of the mother in those features. The bias was like a denial of her. So was the child's obvious preference for her father's caresses.

'Give her a day or two,' Aubrey declared cheerfully. 'You probably won't be able to get rid of her. She'll be all over you.'

The child detached herself from her father and ran out into the garden.

Aubrey paced about the veranda. He paused in front of him. 'Why don't you try to get an interview with the President? I gather he likes talking to foreign journalists. It must flatter his self-esteem to receive international attention.'

Alex, trying his best to look interested, said he would think about it. He sipped the sickly punch; mopped his dripping forehead.

'Why don't you let him relax?' Twirling the gold bracelet looped loosely round her wrist, Dina bestowed on her husband an irritated glance. 'He's only just got off the plane.'

Aubrey fell into an obedient silence.

Smilingly, she turned towards him. 'It's a lot hotter than it should be at this time of year.'

He replied – without any particular regard to truth – that he adored the heat.

The declaration was greeted with the merest lift of an eyebrow. 'Do you really?' Her eyes seemed to laugh at him.

'I worship it.'

She looked away, bending an absent gaze on the child who was standing under the orange-tree peering up intently into its branches from whose inner recesses came a flutter of wings.

'I'm also a heat worshipper,' Aubrey said. 'I never did take to the English climate. It's my opinion that nearly all the fuss Europeans have traditionally made about the unsuitability of tropical climates for their constitutions is a sort of ... well, it's an ideologically motivated prejudice. There is no objective basis for it. It was necessary for the ruling race to draw as many distinctions between themselves and the natives as they could. Physiologically, they can take the heat as well as anybody else. Look at the craze for sunbathing, for getting a tan. One of the major exhibits in my personal museum of colonial attitudes and myths would be the sola topi.'

Dina had had her eyes fixed on him as he spoke. It was an attitude of distant appraisal, aimed not at the words being spoken but at the person of the speaker: a look of puzzled concentration, outwardly patient and complaisant, beneath which, however, Alex thought he could discern the outlines of an exasperation being controlled with difficulty. Infected by her, he found himself looking at rather than listening to Aubrey, endeavouring to see him as she perhaps was seeing him. He saw a man approaching ineffectual middle-age, shorn of any bloom of promise, talking himself into oblivion with a calm, pedantic desperation. What he saw was hurtful and he tried not to see. This exercise in communion with her was a shabby betrayal. He was irked with himself; resentful of her for thus infiltrating his consciousness. He struggled to listen to the words.

Yet, when Aubrey paused, it was to her he addressed himself. 'Don't you like the heat?' he asked.

She hunched her shoulders. 'I have nothing to compare it with so I have no way of knowing.' Twisting her arm, she studied its pale underside.

Aubrey offered more rum punch. He resumed his exposition. 'Just consider the staggering consequences of the belief that only black men were suited for labour in tropical climates. As a result of that myth, millions were uprooted, enslaved, degraded. Today, though, there are white men growing sugar-cane in places like Queensland. Something ought to be written about it.'

'I'm sure something has,' Alex put in – more laconically than he had intended.

Dina, with a peculiar, inward-directed smile, rose and excused herself. She must, she said, go to the kitchen and see how their lunch was progressing. Alex watched her disappear through the doorway.

Aubrey, restored to silence, stirred the liquid in his glass with a finger and licked the sweetness off it. Selma shuffled out of the kitchen doorway, a table-cloth draped over one arm. She started to prepare the table for lunch.

Alex asked the name of the vine covering the back fence.

'We call it Bleeding Heart.' It was Dina who answered the question, her voice sounding behind him as she returned to the veranda.

'What a sinisterly romantic name.'

'It's not at all exotic,' she remarked affably. 'You see it everywhere. Humming birds seem to like the blossom.' She sat down, crossing her legs. Her toe-nails, exposed by her open-work leather slippers, were painted a glossy red; her legs were smoothly shaved.

'Bleeding Heart,' Alex repeated, his attention focussed on the foaming profusion of the vine. 'It puts me in mind of that Oscar Wilde story about the suicidal nightingale. Do you know it?'

She indicated that she did not.

'A nightingale impales herself on the thorn of a rose and feeds it with her heart's blood.'

'And why does she do that?'

'She sacrifices herself for love – so that her beloved can have the reddest of red roses.'

Dina flexed her fingers.

'A voluptuous tale,' Alex said. 'Through the night, while her life oozes away, she sings the sweetest of songs in her scented garden.'

'I have an edition of his collected works in the shop,' Aubrey said. 'Wilde, as you say, is voluptuous. Too voluptuous for my taste anyway.'

Selma rattled cutlery. The bird still flapped and fluttered among the branches of the orange-tree. But Clara had lost interest in it and was now clinging to the skirts of the maid.

'Aubrey tells me you have a degree in English Literature.' Alex watched the play of her flexing fingers, the nails

100

of which – unlike her toes – were unadorned.

. Her lids puckered over narrowed eyes. 'I do. From the University of Cuyama. Whatever that's worth.'

'Come, come.' Aubrey stared at her sorrowfully. 'It's a perfectly good degree in every way.'

'Did you do the Romantics?' Alex asked. 'Keats ...'

She nodded, blinking out into the garden.

'O, for a beaker full of the warm South,
Full of the true, the blushful Hippocrene,
With beaded bubbles winking at the brim,
And purple-stained mouth
That I might drink and leave the world unseen
And with thee fade away into the forest dim ...'

Alex laughed, somewhat amazed at himself. 'Nightingales seem to have a strange effect on the English,' he said. 'Did you like Keats?'

She twirled her bracelet. 'It's a little difficult when you've never heard a nightingale sing. You can't go wandering through *our* forests. We have no violets, no musk roses, no eglantine ...' She smiled at him. 'I'm sure you wouldn't want to fade away into our jungles.'

'I don't agree at all,' Aubrey said. 'It doesn't matter that you've never heard a nightingale sing.'

And he began to talk about the universality of art.

Dina became inert, gazing out into the garden. The shadow of the house was beginning to creep across the grass. Aubrey's voice coiled sonorously, wasting itself in the afternoon stillness.

'Talking of forests dim,' he said at length, 'it's a pity you don't have time to go to the Interior while you are here. Who knows when you might next have the chance?'

'I'm not the rugged, explorer type,' Alex said.

'You don't have to be. Nowadays, it's quite civilised. There are even one or two tourist lodges.' He resumed his pacing of the veranda. 'Even quite a short visit will give you a different perspective on things. It will show you at one and

101

the same time both our enormous backwardness and lack of imagination – *and* our enormous potential.' Aubrey widened his eyes at him.

'I'll think about it,' Alex said. The hunt for 'perspectives' had eaten up his life. He was sick to death of searching for them; he was sick to death of backwardness and potential.

Selma announced lunch.

*

Over lunch Aubrey resumed his monologue on the Plebiscite. Dina did not disguise her lack of interest.

'And what do you make of it?' Alex asked, turning towards her after a decent interval.

'Me?' She appeared taken aback by the question. 'I haven't really given it much thought.'

'You take no interest in politics?'

He saw Aubrey looking at her – intent, mournful.

'Only from a distance. Most of what goes on is way above my head.'

'Politics is best looked at from a distance,' he said lightly, aware of a certain tension in the atmosphere. 'The trouble is that most of it isn't way above the head but way below.'

'That may be so,' Aubrey interrupted. 'But it doesn't make it any the less important. This Plebiscite threatens every aspect of our lives.' He spoke with some heat.

'Is it possible,' she interposed suddenly, 'that people in England are interested in what goes on in a place like Cuyama?' She toyed with a slice of unbuttered bread.

'To be honest – no. Even my editor wasn't too sure where Cuyama was.'

She smiled that inner-directed smile of hers, looking at the child who was being fed bits of salad by her father.

'They forgot about us the moment slavery was abolished and the profits dried up,' Aubrey said.

'And why should they have remembered us?' she asked.

'Because they created the place. None of us would be here

otherwise.' Aubrey scrubbed Clara's messy chin with a napkin.

Dina shrugged. 'So what? Did they ever pretend to be philanthropists?'

'They did indeed! There were those who genuinely believed they were doing the African a great favour by enslaving him, opening his eyes to the truths of Christianity and so saving his benighted soul from eternal damnation.'

'I still don't know what you expect.' She was letting her annoyance show, staring at him almost wrathfully. 'Would you prefer that they shed crocodile tears?'

'All I'm saying is that they bear some responsibility.' He scanned her face warily.

Clara chewed on a piece of lettuce with bovine placidity.

'Responsibility for what exactly?' Her wrathful expression did not abate.

'For the fact that we exist,' Aubrey replied quietly. 'For the fact that we are as we are.'

'But we're supposed to be independent now, aren't we? We're masters of our own fate now, aren't we? It was what we wanted, wasn't it? So why go on begging for attention and sympathy?'

'I'm not begging for attention and sympathy,' Aubrey said.

'Then why write to the editors of all those newspapers?'

Aubrey eased Clara off his knees. She ran off into the house in search of Selma.

'You see,' she went on, turning to Alex and speaking with an unexpectedly malicious emphasis, 'this Plebiscite of ours, about which Aubrey makes such a song and dance, doesn't really matter. Having a Constitution or not having a Constitution won't make the slightest difference to us. We're beyond the reach of that kind of thing.'

Aubrey gazed at her in blank-faced dismay.

Gone was that air of aloof self-control. She rose awkwardly from the table, brushing crumbs off her dress. 'My apologies,' she said. 'I've poked my nose into what is none of my business and ruined your reunion.' She walked off abruptly and disappeared into the house.

*

She went upstairs to the bedroom. Closing the curtains, she lay down on the bed. But she was too restless to sleep and she rose again. She sat down at her dressing table, trying to steady herself. A paperback edition of a Lawrence novel lay amid the scattered combs, hair-brushes, bottles and jars of cosmetics. She picked it up.

'Ah the dark races (she read) . . . the dark races belong to a by-gone cycle of humanity. They are left behind in a gulf out of which they have never been able to climb . . . They can only follow as servants . . .' Her eyes roamed dully to the next paragraph. '. . . let the white man once have a misgiving about his own leadership, and the dark races will at once attack him, to pull him down into the old gulfs.'

Wincing, she let the book fall from her fingers. It was hurtful. It was objectionable. But how different were her own feelings on the matter? Weren't there times when she, child of a dark race, wanted to pull the whole world down with her, to avenge what it had made of her – and all like her? Wasn't she often crazed by the tormenting desire to retaliate?

Every race, Lawrence had said, ought to have its own gods. None but one's own would really do. She thought of that emblematic star, poised between day and night, signalling to the initiated the return of the now juvenescent gods of the Aztecs awakened from their long sleep in the dark places beyond the sun and coming back to reclaim their alienated patrimony. Gods ought to exude out of the pores like sweat. They had to well up from the inside. They could not be borrowed from others or imposed by others. Such gods were no good at all. They had no magic, no potency. Borrowed gods erased the soul and left you with nothing you

could call your own. It was the most terrible form of robbery. Worse, so much worse in the long run, than watching
big machines scoop up the red soil on which you walked
every day and take it away in ships to those lands where it
would be transformed into something called aluminium;
refashioned into gleaming aeroplanes and frying pans.

But where were her gods? Who were they? Christianity
did not belong to her. It had never oozed out of her pores.
She had never experienced the Christian god as a living
presence within her: because he belonged to others, not to
her. All her attempts at prayer had been futile and ridiculous. Her invocations had petered out in an arid silence,
fallen on a ground whose stoniness had appalled her. Nor
could she lay claim to the gods of her father's Hindustani
ancestors. They were utterly dead to her. Nothing could
ever breathe life into those bones. Lawrence was right: but
he was of no help to her – she who had no claim on any
divinity, not on Jesus or Allah or Brahma or Baal or Quet-
zalcoatl. She would have to fabricate her own god. But how
did you do that?

She was formless, lacking a geometry; concocted out of a
primal dust upon which no god had ever stamped its imprint.

'Mallingham,' her father had muttered. 'Mallingham.'

Now she understood.

He had divested himself of everything that he could un-
reservedly lay claim to. Not his religion, not even his name,
could he call his own. Everything had been taken away from
him. He could not have been wholly credible to himself. But
he had had at his disposal no means of expressing his loss
and his resentment. He might scorn his old family name of
Mahalingam, he might laugh at Hindustani superstition and
dirt and backwardness and say that he only 'looked like an
Indian' ... but, all the same, he must also have divined that
his metamorphosis from Mahalingam to Mallingham was not
a transition of which he ought to be especially proud; that in
crossing the no-man's-land from Mahalingam to Mallingham

105

he had not moved from darkness to light but had merely exchanged one kind of defeat for another. He would rage against godlessness because, really, he had no god. Only towards the end had he dared to approach close to the source of his pain, to acknowledge the violation he had suffered.

They had cut themselves off from their country cousins, the descendants of unknown great-uncles and aunts who had resisted the Presbyterian bait; who had remained in their little mud villages buried amid the plains of sugar-cane, who had never ceased worshipping their own gods in their own way; they had cut themselves off from all those country cousins whom she might pass on the street without knowing that their blood and their past was intimately mixed with hers: all those country cousins they had disowned as having nothing in common with them. Conversion, like a knife, had severed the umbilical cord.

How strange it was for Dina Marie Mallingham, daughter of a *Christian* family, the pretty town girl, to remember from time to time those Mahalingams in the cane fields – a sunburnt, rum-soaked, faceless peasantry, hewers of wood, drawers of water, slashing at the sugar-cane with machetes, carrying bundles of grass and firewood on their heads. How strange it was for Dina Marie Mallingham, dreaming over a French or Spanish grammar, to raise her eyes and look around at her own drawing-room and see the yellowing crucifix of ivory piously pinned against the wall between the framed photographs of her mother and father, the vases of carefully arranged flowers, the glass-doored cabinet arrayed with silver-plated knives and forks and the china tea-service, the morris chairs, the piano piled with its books of classical music ... above all the piano – the symbol of their cultural progress and their aspirations.

Naturally enough, the wondrous comparison between Mallingham and Mahalingam came to her only at rare intervals, in rare moods of marvel. Those cousins were too far removed from her; too fabulous an entity. Her father was, for the most part, silent about them, a silence born of discretion and unease rather than active aversion or dislike. It was different from her mother's silence. She, enraptured by that modicum of Portuguese blood flowing in her veins, was neither courteous nor restrained. 'Oh yes,' she had said on one occasion when the subject had come up, 'I keep forgetting you have all those coolie relations.' She had seen her father tauten; she had seen a tremor of protest rise in his throat. But, just as swiftly, he had subsided into quiescence, made no reply and changed the subject.

Now and again, awkward, deferential men turned up at the house, seeking interviews with her father. The aroma of the cane land – of clay, of grass, of earth, of wood-smoke – clung to them. They would bring small offerings with them: mangoes, bananas, tomatoes, papayas – the fruits of the countryside whence they came. Once, one of these men had lifted her on to his lap and given her a stick of sugar-cane. Her father met them on the veranda. There they talked. Beyond that point in the house they never penetrated. These conferences were conducted in a muted buzz. Her father did not divulge much. 'Mind your own business,' he would reply if questioned by her or any other of the children. Perhaps, there was not a great deal to divulge.

Once, with greater boldness than usual, he had unexpectedly said, 'It might be interesting to go down to Cuyuni one of these days. See a different type of life.' She had been attracted by the idea. 'Yes, Papa,' she had said, 'let's do that.' But Grace had squawked with disgust; and Mona and Alice had not shown the slightest interest. The indiscreet offer had not been repeated. Dina suspected that, from time to time, her father did make secret visits to Cuyuni. However, she had no proof of this until much later.

Yet, how glad, how thankful she was, that her name was Dina Marie Mallingham. At school, Hindustani names, Hindustani food, Hindustani customs, Hindustani gods and goddesses, always gave rise to hilarity. Even the teachers had participated in the mockery. There was that terrible day when a slight, dark-skinned country girl, dumb with anxiety, had inexplicably surfaced among them in the middle of one term. Her name was Phulbassie Mahalingam. 'I don't think I'll ever be able to pronounce that,' the teacher had said, having not made the smallest effort to do so. By lunch-time she had been saddled with the nickname 'Cooliebassie' – and she was in tears. Dina Marie Mallingham would have liked to befriend her, but she had lacked the courage. Phulbassie Mahalingam had been left to fend for herself as best she could. That night her father said, 'I believe you have a new girl in your class.' 'Yes, Papa – but how did you know?' He smiled, shaking his head, hesitating before adding, 'Try and be nice to her.' The shame of her betrayal had nagged at her for a long time afterwards. Even now, recalling it, the shame returned.

Sitting at the dressing-table, she buried her face in her hands and tried not to think about it.

*

It was Alex who broke the silence. 'I hope it wasn't anything I said. That remark about people in England not knowing where Cuyama was and not being interested . . . hardly very tactful.'

Aubrey roused himself. 'Dina wouldn't take offence at such remarks. I can assure you of that.' Aubrey picked up the bread-knife, squinting at his reflection in the blade. 'She's been very overwrought these past few weeks. Whether we care to admit it or not, this Plebiscite has been a terrible strain on all of us. It's as if there's some virus floating about. None of us are quite ourselves.' He smiled tiredly, toying with the bread-knife, running a finger along the edge of the blade, frowning at his reflection.

Alex let the languor of the afternoon flow over him. The shadow of the house now occupied nearly half of the garden and the light was yellower. How much of his explanation did Aubrey believe? Could his wife's contempt, so nakedly expressed, have escaped him? Surely not even Aubrey could be so blind. Pity was awakened in him.

'Would you like to inspect the bookshop?'

Alex, shaking himself into wakefulness, said he would like nothing better. He followed Aubrey into the dark shop. The fluorescent lighting crackled and sparked into life.

'My little kingdom,' Aubrey said, spreading wide his arms.

Alex looked round the small, square room in the centre of which, altar-like, was Aubrey's roll-top desk. Above the varnished shelves built along each of the walls was a quotation, rendered in black lettering, praising books, those who wrote them and those who sold them.

In The Best Books Great Men Talk To Us, Give Us Their Most Precious Thoughts, And Pour Their Souls Into Ours.

People Die But Books Never Die.

Dreams, Books, Are Each A World.

For I Bless God In The Libraries Of The Learned And For All the Booksellers In The World.

Alex scanned the array of forbidding titles filling the shelves. He picked up a treatise on peasant cooperatives in Colombia.

'A highly quixotic selection,' Aubrey observed with a smile.

'You aim at the university market, do you?' Alex replaced the book on peasant cooperatives and pulled out another – a study of the destabilisation campaign waged by the United States against Allende's Chile: he was foraging in the Latin American section.

'Our university students can't afford to buy many books.'

'Then . . .'

Aubrey laughed. 'Very few ever get sold. Mainly foreigners buy – people working with the embassies and so on. But they buy mainly novels.'

Overhead, the fluorescent tubes crackled, dimmed, re-covered their vigour.

'I keep it going as a matter of principle. It's a gesture of faith. You probably think it's foolish. Most people do. A waste of good money – though one should bear in mind that Cuyamese money is not much good for anything outside Cuyama.'

Alex did not say anything. He would have liked to ask what Dina thought about it. The question was on the tip of his tongue. But he desisted. He picked up and restored to its place a history of Botswana – he had shifted his explorations from Latin America to the Africa, South of the Sahara section.

Aubrey, taking a bunch of keys from his trouser-pocket, opened one of the desk drawers and extracted from it a brown, loose-leaf folder.

'My one hundred pages of fictional creation,' he said, weighing the folder in his palms. 'Started five years ago. Abandoned one year later. Can you think of a sadder epi-taph?' He leafed through the typescript, blowing away the dust which had collected on the pages. 'Dreams are such cruel things, Alex. Afflictions of the soul. Once they get hold of you, you are never really able to get rid of them. They are like ghosts that never let you alone. With what high hopes I came back to Cuyama. I remember I couldn't sleep on the last night of the voyage – I travelled home by boat. I spent all night on deck, leaning against the rails, staring at the Cuyamese coast.

'It wasn't simply the excitement of returning home that prevented me from sleeping. It was another kind of excite-ment. I was thinking of all my assorted ambitions for this place. I was going to help it make something of itself, put myself at its disposal, expiate the sins of my slave-owning forefathers. I was going to help it transcend its cruel history, wash its wounds. It sounds ridiculous, I know. But that's how it was. I saw myself a teacher, an exemplar, an illuminator of men's minds.'

Aubrey stopped speaking. He closed the dusty folder, weighing those hundred pages of effort in the scales of his palms, glancing round the shop with its mocking array of books that would never be sold and never be read.

'You know what I am called? I'm called the holy fool. The title was conferred by a cousin of mine. She and Dina are good friends.' Fleetingly, something like bitterness darkened his face.

Alex stared helplessly at him.

Aubrey laughed. 'All of which reminds me – I have a little present for you.' He opened another drawer of the desk and took from it a slim pile of magazines. 'One of my earlier ventures,' he explained, blowing and slapping the dust off the covers. '*Unchained* was to be Cuyama's great journal of literary and political expression, a forum open to all the talents. It too didn't work out quite as I had planned.' He handed over the collection. 'Still, you may find some useful background material in it.'

They made their way back to the garden, almost the whole of which was now in shade. The table had been cleared of all traces of their lunch. A rattle of crockery came from the kitchen where Selma was doing the washing-up.

'I'll walk you over to the hotel,' Aubrey said. 'You've had a long day. You must be exhausted. I'll go and tell Dina.'

'Don't disturb her on my account.'

But Aubrey went in search of her all the same.

Apart from the noises Selma made in the kitchen, the yellow afternoon was stamped with a dead stillness. Alex stared at the Bleeding Heart.

Dina appeared in the doorway. She crossed the veranda, moving towards him with an easy, swinging gait. Her face looked strained and sallow but, in general, she seemed to have regained her composure. She glanced down at the magazines he was holding.

'A present from Aubrey,' he said.

Aubrey joined them. He was carrying Alex's suitcase.

111

They walked through the house out to the veranda at the front. She leaned against the railing, watching them go down the steps lined with potted ferns.

As they were about to pass through the gate, Aubrey suggested that Dina might show Alex the sights of Charlestown.

Alex made demurring noises.

'There isn't a great deal to see,' she said, looking down at him. 'But I'd be more than happy to show you what there is.'

'I was telling Alex about those statues they have piled up in the Botanical Gardens. Or you could take him to the old fort. That is something he shouldn't miss.'

Alex continued to make demurring noises.

'It really doesn't put me out in the slightest,' she said. 'I have nothing much to do – I'm a lady of leisure.'

Aubrey rubbed his hands, looking up gratefully at his wife.

Chapter Eight

She watched them walk up the street. Alex, several inches taller, several inches broader, dwarfed Aubrey. They turned right by the church and disappeared. She lingered on the veranda, leaning against the railing, looking out at the empty street. The leaves of the trees and bushes in the churchyard were motionless. A golden haze of dust obscured the remoter vistas of Independence Park. The image of the playing-card she had seen lying in the gutter returned to her.

She retreated into the sitting room, furnished in the main with old, heavy pieces of furniture passed on to them by Stephanie St Pierre. The walls were decorated with the works of local artists: Aubrey considered it his duty to patronise their efforts. She looked round dully at the portraits of gnarled black women, gnarled black men; at a beach scene and a jungle landscape.

They hardly ever used this room, a mausoleum of St Pierre grandeur. Her gaze strayed over an elaborately carved folding screen, a low table inlaid with ivory arabesques standing in front of the sofa, brass lamps with tasselled shades, mahogany bookcases. Odd ... Aubrey's combination of piety and revolt. She was alienated from both these aspects of his character. After several years of marriage, the St Pierres remained strangers to her. With the single exception of Beatrice, his first cousin, she had never ceased to feel herself an interloper. These relics, on which Stephanie St Pierre had set such great store, aroused no emotion in her, serving only to emphasise her estrangement.

'How I envy you getting hold of those things,' Beatrice had remarked. 'I'd give my eye-teeth for some of those pieces you have there.'

To which Dina had replied: 'If they were mine to dispose of, Beatie, you could take them all away this instant.'

Beatrice had not really understood and she had not tried to explain.

'Darling,' Beatrice had said, 'it's clear you don't have an inkling of their value. On the Portobello Road they'd go mad over that stuff.'

Dina had merely smiled and let it go at that.

She stood there, looking round the room. She could have been a trespasser who, quite by chance, had wandered into an unknown house and become trapped there. The room seemed to heave beneath her. She swayed, as if about to fall, and clutched at a chair for support. Her palms were moist, her heart pounded. She closed her eyes and clenched her teeth. The sensation faded away.

She walked out to the veranda at the back. What was there to be so afraid of? She saw herself a corpse abandoned, covered with moss and mud. Looking up at the smouldering hills, another wave of objectless fear rolled over her.

'Selma! Are you still here, Selma?' She was reassured by the sound of her own voice.

Selma appeared in the kitchen doorway.

Dina gazed foolishly at her. 'I was just wondering if you were still here.'

'You want something?'

'No. I don't want anything.'

She examined the face of this unfriendly black girl with whom she had exchanged so few words; about whom she knew so little. To Selma, Dina had only spoken words of command. She was Aubrey's protegée and she did not interfere in their dealings with each other. Selma was not supposed to be a 'servant', Aubrey being allergic to that des-

114

cription of her status. Yet, if Selma wasn't a servant – what was she?

Aubrey had found her up in the hills and brought her to live with them. This had happened about a year after they were married.

'Someone like Selma will be very useful to have around the place,' he said.

'I thought,' she replied, 'you are against having servants.'

Aubrey looked shocked. 'Selma isn't going to be treated as a servant,' he said.

'What is she going to be treated as?'

Aubrey had been characteristically vague. 'The idea is to help her make something of herself,' he said, 'to expose her to a different kind of environment. Up there in the hills, she doesn't stand a chance. You must know by now that I'm something of an environmental determinist. As for what she'll do, she can help you out around the house and perform a few simple tasks for me in the bookshop – just dusting the books, for instance, will be a great help.'

'Another assistant!' She had laughed. Aubrey had looked embarrassed.

Selma moved in.

Whether or not Selma had come any nearer to making something of herself during the four years she had spent with them was debatable. Aubrey, to begin with, had insisted that Selma eat at table with them: an indulgence which scandalised Stephanie St Pierre. These exercises in egalitarianism were a disaster. Selma, head bowed obdurately over her plate, seemed to lose her appetite. In the end, Selma pleaded to be allowed to take her food in the kitchen. Aubrey had conceded defeat gracefully.

Selma disappointed in other directions. Charles Dickens, even in the simplified and abridged versions supplied to her by Aubrey, was rejected in favour of the romantic comic-books she smuggled into the house.

When Selma, at the age of sixteen, announced that she

was with child, Aubrey merely sighed. Selma's mother was more forthright: she arrived wailing at the house and beat her daughter with a broom. Aubrey, somehow, managed to procure her an abortion. After that, without saying so, it was clear that he had given up on her. Selma was allowed to slide into the status of servant – though the term itself continued to be withheld. She had to be added to that list of high-minded projects which had got nowhere.

Dina, for some reason she did not clearly understand, had never really taken to the girl; nor did Selma seem to take to her. It was a mutual dislike which neither had exerted herself to remedy. If Aubrey noticed this, he chose to do nothing about it. From time to time, one of Selma's brothers – who, of late, had begun to cultivate a Rastafarian hairstyle – turned up at the house and pretended to work in the garden. Once or twice a month, Selma's crippled wreck of a mother, her swollen legs bandaged in filthy rags, showed up and wheedled various favours and donations out of Aubrey. He had, in fact, more or less taken Selma's family under his wing and – Dina was convinced – was being shamelessly exploited by them. Aubrey, however, was not one to advertise his acts of charity.

Selma behaved like most of her kind. She stole food, experimented with Dina's cosmetics, appropriated the odd blouse and skirt and assorted items of underwear. Recently, these thefts had become bolder as well as more frequent. Dina, on principle, never complained. But this tolerance did not make Selma like her any better. Dina had begun to suspect that these plunderings were motivated not only by the desire for possession but had become Selma's chosen way of taunting her, of challenging her to do or say something. This had strengthened her passivity which, in due course, had become *her* way of challenging and taunting Selma. So it was that, without anything being said, servant and mistress had warred with one another; and Dina hated it and hated herself for doing it. This dishonourable combat of will with a creature from the slums symbolised for her the aridity – the poison – which was eating away her life and deforming her existence.

Now, looking at the unfriendly girl, she made an effort to smile.

'You have a boyfriend, Selma?'

Selma jerked her shoulders. Her cheeks puffed out truculently.

'Is he,' Dina persisted, 'that man I've seen you talking to? The one who comes on the bicycle?' She had observed these furtive encounters from her bedroom window.

Selma narrowed her eyes. Her servant's mentality, anticipating accusations and interdictions, reacted defensively. 'He don't come in the house. I never let him come inside. We always talk with one another out on the street. We don't come in your house to talk.'

'I'm not accusing you or objecting to anything,' Dina replied. She sought to maintain her air of charitable curiosity. 'I only wanted to know if he was your boyfriend.'

Selma, cheeks puffed out, did not relax her guard. 'I suppose you could call him that,' she said.

'Have you known him a long time?'

'Not all that long.' The words oozed reluctantly from her lips.

'You would like to marry him?'

Selma jerked her shoulders. Dina recoiled from the bristling hostility. Still, having committed herself to this show of interest, she persisted.

'Wouldn't you like to marry him?'

'I not sure he's the marrying kind.'

An uneasy silence intervened, during which Selma looked not at her mistress but at a point in space a few inches above her head. Dina studied the smooth, purple-black face swollen with sullenness. She had not always been as morose, as slatternly as this. Aubrey might talk and talk and talk, write and write and write. But, for instance, what did a free press

117

matter to someone like Selma? What use would she have for it? Selma's ideals were mysteries to them. They saw only the servant aspect of her. Within that head might be whirling visions and lusts which, if suddenly unbared, might astonish them. Confronted with Selma's unavowed urges (did she ever fantasise about murdering them in their beds?), even Aubrey's complacent compassion might shrink back on itself. Yet, what right did she have to be contemptuous about Selma? What, after all, were *her* ideals? Maybe she didn't have any. Or, maybe, she didn't care to know. If Aubrey could have opened up her head and seen what was inside, she too might have made his compassion shrink back on itself.

'How old are you now, Selma?'

'I have eighteen years.'

'So – you can vote.' Dina fabricated a smile. 'Do you plan to vote in the Plebiscite?'

Selma's sullenness intensified. She moved her shoulders enigmatically, slowly scratching her arm. Her nails left whitened trails on her skin.

'If you voted, would you support the President?'

Sullenness congealed into defiance. Her mulish ambiguity was not hard to interpret.

'You disagree with Mr Aubrey ...'

Selma stared at her.

Dina laughed. 'Tell me something, Selma. Why don't you like me?'

Selma, immobile, expressionless now, fixed her attention on the point in space. 'Is you who don't like me.' Her voice was barely audible.

'Why shouldn't I like you?' Dina tried to seem amused.

Selma lowered her gaze. Briefly, their eyes met. Dina looked away.

'Is Mr Aubrey who bring me here,' Selma said. 'I never asked to come.'

Dina nodded. 'That is quite true. Do you like Mr Aubrey, Selma?'

'I have nothing against Mr Aubrey.'

'But do you like him?'

Selma's eyes dilated reflectively. 'Mr Aubrey tries to be a good man. He never do me any harm.'

'Have I done you harm?'

Selma did not answer.

'That's all right, Selma. You can go now. Thank you for talking to me.'

Selma headed back towards the kitchen. On reaching the doorway, she paused. With deliberation, she turned round to consider her mistress. 'One day,' she said, 'black people going to rule the world. You hear me?'

'I hear you, Selma.'

'Black people ain't going to be slaves no more. We done with that.'

'I hear you, Selma.'

Selma vanished into the kitchen.

When she had gone, Dina stepped down from the veranda and paced slowly about the garden.

*

Life – her life – had finally been sucked dry of its charms. Whatever sweetness it might once have had, whatever fascination, seemed to have been squeezed out of it. She had depleted her reserves of energy, of inspiration, of hope. Only bitterness dripped and dribbled out of her. She had come to the end of her modest little road.

Tracing its windings, she saw that it had never promised to lead anywhere in particular. No specific destination had ever been sign-posted. It had wound desultorily from childhood to adolescence, from adolescence to the university, from the university to long months of idleness culminating in her acceptance of the job of 'assistant' offered by Aubrey in his bookshop, from that to marriage, from marriage to childbirth, from an aborted motherhood to *this*. Now there was nowhere else for it to go. It had taken her as far as it could.

That road had wound its way through a featureless countryside offering at no juncture even the ghost of a majestic view; it had taken her across a stony and sterile plain that could nourish nothing, shelter nothing but the meanest vegetable growth. The scattered milestones she had encountered along the way charted not her progress but her frustrations and failures and surrenders. And what had she been looking for? What had she been hoping for? She had never been able to say. Yet she could neither disown nor disregard the restlessness which had descended on her from she knew not where. It was a restlessness compounded out of dissatisfaction, yearning and – the most prominent ingredient of all – terror. A terror that had no definite shape. A terror whose source and meaning eluded her. A terror of shadows; of the formless night. Perhaps *this* was the terror, she thought as she lay prone on the easy chair, looking towards the scraggy orange-tree, its branches scaly, its bark whitened by some fungus, whose scant fruits were always inedible. Long before they had ripened, the oranges would fall and rot away on the ground. *This* was the terror – finding herself as she was now, with no indication that there was any more road ahead of her. The terror of finding yourself aborted; your fruit rotten before it had had a chance to ripen and yield its sweetness.

'I really can't for the life of me understand why you think yourself so special,' Grace had once sneered at her. 'You seem to believe that some Prince Charming is going to come riding up one day and take you away on his white horse.' She smiled at the memory. No Prince Charming had ever appeared on a white horse offering to take her away with him. Aubrey, whatever else he might be, was not Prince Charming. She had let herself be married to him because she saw no alternative; because she was desperate not for a husband but for herself. Because the act of marriage would, for a while at any rate, push forward the winding road of her life. At that moment it had been in imminent peril of petering out, of leaving her stranded in the middle of nowhere. Later, seeking a further reprieve, she had let herself become a mother. Marriage and motherhood had extended the road through the wilderness for a few more miles. How was that road to be continued?

It was not that she craved some glorious, cloud-capped fulfilment. What she craved was a sense of motion; a vision of the road ahead. That was all. She jerked herself out of the easy chair and began to pace the tiled length of the veranda. She refused to concede that her life could grind to a halt just like that. There had to be a little touch of rhyme somewhere; a little touch of reason. She looked out over the shaded garden. A rosy light brightened the slopes of the hills. She imagined she could hear Aubrey tapping away at his typewriter in the bookshop. The halting tap tap of his two-fingered technique insinuated itself into her consciousness. It took possession of it, making of her skull an echo chamber. Tap tap tap ... She clapped her hands over her ears.

Chapter Nine

When Aubrey returned from the hotel, he found her in the deck chair. She was reading. He came and stood behind the chair, hands in pockets, looking up at the smoking hills.

'Is he safely installed?' She spoke without taking her eyes off the book.

'Yes – though, needless to say, there was some confusion about the booking.'

She said: 'I'm sorry about what happened over lunch.'

'Never mind. As I was telling Alex, we're all overwrought. None of us are quite ourselves these days.'

Dina frowned. If she had made Selma the victim of her tolerance, Aubrey had made her, Dina, the victim of his.

'How do you suppose Selma will vote in the Plebiscite?' she asked.

'I expect she won't vote at all. I doubt she even knows what the issues are.'

'But – let us assume she understands the issues – where do you think her sympathies would lie?' She peered interestedly at him.

'You know . . . (he laughed – somewhat embarrassed by the admission he was about to make) . . . it hasn't even occurred to me to find out. I must have a chat with her.'

'I thought you attached great importance to the sound political education of the masses.'

'I do. You're quite justified in rebuking me. I've been very remiss.' He gazed guiltily at her.

'Do you believe a free press matters to someone like Selma?'

'A free press matters to everybody.' Recovering himself, he assumed a tutorial expression.

'What are your plans for her? She's no longer a child, you know. She even has the vote now.'

'I'm afraid it's something I haven't given much thought to recently. But why do you ask? Why this sudden interest in Selma?'

'I was just wondering. I don't expect she wants to stay on here indefinitely.'

'No, I don't expect she does.' Aubrey stroked his beard. 'A shame it didn't work out as I'd hoped it would.' He sighed. 'I'll have a talk with her. By the way, I hope you didn't mind my suggesting you show Alex around.'

'Not at all. Why should I mind? It's one way of passing the time.' She went on reading.

'It's taking you a long time to get through that Lawrence,' he said.

'Yes.'

She could feel him standing there behind her, debating with himself, wanting to say or ask something.

'Do you remember how wonderful it was in Italy that time? Coming out of the railway station at Venice, seeing the Grand Canal right there before your very eyes. You couldn't believe it was the real thing – do you remember?'

'I remember.'

'And do you remember that hotel we stayed in overlooking the lake? I woke up in the middle of the night and saw you sitting by the window. At first I thought something was wrong. But there was nothing wrong. You were admiring the moon on the water. And how extraordinarily beautiful it was! Do you remember?'

'I remember.'

'We should do something like that again – a second honeymoon.' His eyes rested on her with timid solicitation.

She shook her head slowly, blinking into the glare of the afternoon. She could feel him wanting to touch her.

His fingers drummed on the metal frame of the deck chair.

'I don't want to go to Europe,' she said.

The drumming ceased. 'Why not?' he asked after a pause.

'What have I got to do with Europe? What's Europe got to do with someone like me? All those paintings, all those museums, all those palaces ... no ... no ...'

'I don't understand you,' he murmured.

'Civilisation passed me by,' she said.

'I hate to hear you talk like that.'

'You may hate it,' she said, pulling herself upright. 'And I may hate it. But it doesn't make it any the less true because of that. Unpleasant facts have to be faced.'

'Civilisation doesn't belong to any one race or culture. It belongs to all of us.' He waved his arms. 'Shakespeare and Goethe and Raphael are universal. They belong to all of us.'

'I know ... I know ... That's what I used to believe – or used to pretend I believed. But it's not true. It's a lie. All those famous people you mentioned have nothing to say to me and I have nothing to say to them. It may be different for you, for Beatrice. But for me ...' She stared stubbornly away from him.

'Newton's laws of gravity are the same for an Englishman as they are for us.'

She laughed.

He left her and went into the bookshop.

*

He stood in the twilight of the shuttered shop, looking at the shelves of pristine books: his virginal soldiers drawn up in battle array on the varnished wood. The Sunday silence hummed in his ears. He sat down at the roll-top desk and buried his head in his hands.

Nearly everything to which he had put his hands had turned to dust. After all the effort, he had so little to show: a bookshop whose precarious commercial performance had pushed it to the verge of bankruptcy; two dozen articles of

124

indifferent quality and interest; a handful of short stories, overwrought exercises in 'social realism'; a few back numbers of that impossibly slim magazine he had called *Unchained* – a magazine written largely by himself, which had died a sudden and undignified death; a novel which he had begun a dozen times and abandoned a dozen times.

All of these disappointments he could – and did – explain away. He could say that the bookshop was what it was because of the high prices he was forced to charge simply to break even, because the country was still in its intellectual infancy and could not tell a good book from a bad one, because, considering the high prices he had to pay, he could afford only a limited stock. He could say that his magazine had folded because of the excessive duties levied by the Government on newsprint, because of the scarcity of advertisers, because many of its would-be contributors were intimidated into silence by the informal censorship and their fears of equally informal reprisal. All of which was true. They could be explained; and out of explanation would come consolation and renewed endeavour. He could be stoical about them. They could be interpreted as part of the larger battle he had elected to fight.

His marriage, however, stood out. Unlike all the rest, it could not be explained away. He had, to the best of his ability, been a good husband – a considerate and sympathetic and loyal husband, who had never demanded more from his wife than she was capable of giving or was willing to give. He had left her free to follow her own inclinations, to be whatever she wanted to be; or, as he had put it, to 'realise' herself.

But what were those inclinations? What did she want to be? To those questions Aubrey still had no answers. She had not provided any.

'Are you telling me,' she had asked in one of her more mischievous moods, 'that you won't object to anything I might do?'

'Within reason,' he replied. 'Everything within reason.'

'And what does reason forbid?' she asked.

'Think rather of what it allows,' he countered jovially.

'What does it allow?'

His response to that challenge had been vague. 'Why – you could try and write,' he exclaimed. He had been inspired by that vision of her which had unexpectedly presented itself to him. 'Why don't you try putting pen to paper? See what you come up with. What do you have to lose? You might surprise yourself.'

'What would you have me write about?' she enquired.

'*I* wouldn't have you write about anything in particular,' he said. 'Your subject matter you'll have to discover for yourself. You could write children's stories, for example. Cuyama has some splendid folk tales on which you could base them. Or, you could try your hand at a novel. You know what they say – everybody has at least one novel in them.'

He had poured out his ideas at her, ideas to which she had listened but not responded.

For he had had a high idea of her intelligence and natural gifts; of what he liked to describe as her 'human possibility'. Perhaps it was that exaggerated vision which, from the beginning, had drawn him to her. He had made it his self-appointed duty to bring it to light. He had wanted to be the humble agency of its self-fulfilment. It was that nebulous human possibility with which he had fallen in love. He had transformed her into a personification of his optimism. She was his idealism made flesh. 'Your sweetness,' he had declared during the early days, 'must not be wasted on the desert air.'

She had looked at him as if he were mad.

Now that passionate optimism was all but dead. Dina remained a mystery to him.

Off and on she helped him out in the bookshop – filling in for him during his absences, assisting with the accounts, giving desultory advice about the choice of books to be stocked. Generally, though, she performed these tasks without enthusiasm. She seemed to have no real interest in either the aims or the fate of the Aurora – or, come to that, in any of those things which lay closest to his heart. He could not break through the wall of reserve she had erected around herself. Prolonged observation of her only served to emphasise her opacity.

She avoided his circle of friends – the cream, as he saw it, of Cuyamese intellectual society – and, impervious to his constant prodding, took little or no part in their weekly gatherings on the back veranda. Mostly, she spent her days in idleness, sitting out in the garden reading novels, sleeping or merely staring into space. Her lethargy had always astonished him.

The one person she had time for, whose company, it seemed, never staled, was Beatrice; and Aubrey did not approve of his cousin whose 'dolce vita' affectations were quite out of place in Cuyama. From the first Beatrice had shown an unhealthy interest in his wife.

'I'll supervise the re-education of your delectable virgin,' she had said to Aubrey at their wedding lunch in the ball room of the Park Hotel. 'I'll tease her out of her shell.'

'I'm afraid you'll be disappointed,' he had said. 'You'll soon find that Dina isn't at all your type.'

Beatrice, slightly drunk or pretending to be slightly drunk, had giggled. 'Don't you believe it, darling.' She glanced towards Dina who was talking to her mother-in-law. 'Would you like to take a bet on it?'

'No,' Aubrey replied. 'I'm not a betting man.'

As it was, he had been proved wrong. It had taken Dina no time at all to fall under the spell of his first cousin, so often mentioned in the gossip column of the newspaper. If Aubrey was tempted to blame anyone for the disappointments and anti-climactic nature of his marriage, he was inclined to blame Beatrice. It was under her influence, he felt, that Dina had begun to slip away from him; to drift further and further from the ideal lodged in his imagination.

The birth of their child, his last hope of a miracle – granted she had no desires he could detect, was it too much to expect the joys of motherhood to rush in and fill the vacuum? – had not altered this state of affairs. It merely added another link to the chain of his disappointments. At home, the child spent most of its time with Selma. When Clara was not being tended by Selma, she was being looked after by his mother.

'There are times,' Stephanie St Pierre had said to her son, 'when I feel this child is more mine than Dina's.'

Aubrey, despite knowing that sooner or later his mother was bound to raise the delicate subject, flinched when the moment finally did come. He looked down at his sandalled feet.

'Doesn't Dina want to be with her child?' she asked. 'Her behaviour isn't natural, you know. Not natural at all.'

Aubrey remained silent, torn between the temptation to discuss his distress and his reluctance to talk about his wife behind her back. He was opposed to conspiracies of intimate revelation. Observing at a distance the get-togethers of Beatrice and Dina had confirmed that aversion. Yet, even at that moment, Clara was crawling about her grandmother's house, her mother nowhere in sight.

'Surely,' Stephanie St Pierre went on, keeping her eyes fixed on his lowered head, 'a child should be with its mother. It needs its mother. And that poor child, when she's not here with me, who is she with? She's being brought up by a servant. Even you must see that's wrong.'

Even him!

'Haven't you spoken to Dina?' she asked, adopting a gentler tone.

'You do her an injustice,' Aubrey said at last. 'It's not true to say that Selma does everything for Clara when she's not staying with you. You make it sound as if Dina does nothing at all.'

But to himself he put the question: what did Dina actually do with the child? She kissed her in the mornings when Selma presented her at the breakfast table; she might, if she were in the mood, feed her bits of bread, wipe her stained mouth, voice the odd endearment; calling for brush and comb, she might even rearrange her hair. Clara would then disappear with Selma for the rest of the day, following her around the house, accompanying her on shopping expeditions. At her bed-time, Dina would reappear to provide more kisses and endearments.

Nevertheless there were days when she ignored the child altogether, when Clara's presence appeared to cause her only irritation. She would summon Selma. 'Can't you *do* something with this child?' she would demand.

This child.

It pained Aubrey to hear her speak of Clara in that way.

Whenever he could, he brought Clara with him into the bookshop. The child roused an agony of tenderness in him. This was aggravated when he heard her crying deep in the night and, with Dina unresponsive to her wails, hurried to her room. There he would offer what solace he could until she fell asleep.

'Come now, Aubrey,' Stephanie St Pierre said. 'You may have your head in the clouds. But you're not blind.'

Aubrey grimaced, not daring to look directly at his mother. 'Dina's probably suffering from a form of post-natal depression,' he hazarded.

Stephanie St Pierre snorted.

Aubrey clung to his hypothesis. 'It's a well-documented phenomenon, Mother. Not something I've invented.'

'It's all nonsense and you know it.'

Aubrey sighed. 'It really isn't as bad as you say, Mother. Dina may not conform to the archetypal image of a mother. But then many modern women don't. Times have changed. Women are beginning to see themselves in a different light. Sexual stereotyping is breaking down. In Europe and America ...'

His mother broke into the smooth flow. 'We were talking about Dina. Your wife. Remember?'

Dina. His wife. Aubrey remembered. He realised that he was failing to convince even himself; that words did not lessen his pain.

Aubrey, staring at his sandalled feet, wagged his head. 'You must recognise,' he said miserably, 'that not everyone is the same. We cannot expect others to be exactly like us or exactly like we would want them to be. We live in an imperfect world.' He glanced up at the sky, radiant with stars. 'There're some who will always remain mysteries. It's no good crying over that. They have different ways of doing things, different needs, different ways of expressing their ... expressing their love.' A film of melancholy dimmed his eyes; and still he refused to look directly at his mother.

He was aware of her watching him intently: he was like an insect trapped inside a bottle, vainly, frantically, whirring and beating its wings in a delirium of desperation, hurling its impotent body against the walls of its prison.

'Do you believe your own nonsense, Aubrey? Do you honestly believe the sort of things you've been saying to me? Look at me.'

He did not look at her. 'I make a principle of believing everything I say, Mother. You should know that by now.'

'Then you're a fool, my son.'

The accusation was sufficiently familiar, sufficiently well-intentioned, for Aubrey not to be offended. Without knowing why, despite himself, he said: 'Dina isn't a monster, you know.'

Lightly, she brushed the sleeves of his smock with a dark, bejewelled finger.

He offered up those walks to the Botanical Gardens with Clara as evidence of his wife's reformation.

'One swallow doesn't make a summer,' Stephanie St Pierre said.

'You're very difficult to please, Mother.' He smiled at her.

How could he explain to her that, so far as his wife was concerned, even one swallow could provide him with an occasion for subdued rejoicing? How could he begin to explain to her what he was barely able to admit to himself – that he no longer believed in summer?

*

He became slowly aware of the spectral figure standing in the curtained doorway gazing upon him as he sat hunched at the desk. How long had she been standing there, looking in upon him? He straightened himself, displeased at being discovered in that posture of utter dejection.

'Selma,' he said.

She was dressed in her Sunday best: maroon, pleated skirt reaching to her knees, white, long-sleeved blouse buttoned at the wrist (he recognised it as one of Dina's – it had disappeared some weeks before), blunt-toed shoes of mock patent leather. Pendent earrings glinted. Her face was ghostly with powder. A small, imitation snakeskin handbag dangled from her wrist. She reeked of some cheap scent. Each Sunday, garbed in all her finery, Selma returned to her family up in the hills, coming back to them on Monday evening.

'I going now,' Selma said. She remained motionless.

He understood what was required of him: this was Selma's way of asking for her money, for the 'allowance' he gave her at the end of each week. Automatically, he pulled open one of the desk drawers and took out the cash-box. Automatically, aware of the girl's eyes fixed on his fingers, he counted out the worn notes and handed them to her. Selma folded them away into her handbag of imitation snakeskin. With an expression of mild distaste, he studied the thickly powdered face, the meretricious glitter of the earrings, the pleated maroon skirt falling just below the knee. She had become a full-blown woman almost without him noticing it; a creature distinct from the child, her hair plaited into tiny pigtails,

131

whom, on impulse, he had taken from her mother and brought down from the hills to live with them. Her mother, burdened with more children than she knew what to do with, had happily surrendered responsibility to him. As ever, he had had a bright vision which he had proved incapable of making real. The girl from the hills seemed to symbolise all the futility of his endeavours.

'Have you had any thoughts about the future?' He gazed wearily at her.

Her cheeks puffed out.

'You mustn't misunderstand me,' he said. 'I'm not trying to get rid of you.' He looked round the twilit room, breathing in the bookish odours. A dusty beam of late-afternoon light slanted in through the strip of glass above the street door. He rose from the chair. Hands clasped behind his back, he paced about the room. 'It's just that I can't read the future too well myself. I don't know what's going to happen. Everything is most uncertain. It's possible that I may even have to close down the bookshop. You must know that we don't sell too many books.' He stopped speaking, running his eyes along the shelves.

She watched him, mute, unbending.

'I'm not trying to drive you away. I'm only trying to . . . to face unpleasant facts. I've spent the best years of my life chasing after the figments of my imagination. You were a figment of my imagination – just like all the rest. It's only now I'm beginning to see what everybody else saw a long time ago. When it came down to it, I couldn't do the simplest things. I couldn't even teach you to read and write! I couldn't even do that! I took you away from your home and when you didn't conform to my expectations, I abandoned you.'

She watched him, mute, unforgiving.

He stopped her as she was pushing her way through the beaded curtain. 'I'll drive you home,' he said. 'I need some fresh air.'

Dina had disappeared from the back veranda. He went

upstairs in search of her. The shower was going in the bathroom.

'I'm taking Selma home,' he said. 'Would you like to come for the drive?'

Her muffled reply indicated that she would not.

He looked round the bedroom that was theirs. Her clothes were flung casually on the bed. On top of them was the Lawrence novel. Her cosmetics were ranked neatly on her dressing table. He considered these scattered relics. Their intimacy belied the fragile nature of her presence in his life: a presence that resembled a permanent state of absence. She had given so little of herself to him. He picked up her blouse and crushed it against his face. Astonished at himself, he let it slip from his fingers and fall back on the bed.

He hastened downstairs. Selma was waiting for him on the pavement.

*

He felt better in the car.

'Look,' Selma said.

He looked and saw clouds of smoke rising distantly above the rooftops.

'Fire,' Selma said. She spoke with an air of contentment. 'It must be one of those Syrian stores downtown,' she added.

Bit by bit Charlestown was being razed to the ground. Extensive tracts of the city had been reduced to rubble. In many of these empty spaces little stalls and shacks had sprung up. Month by month, the colonial town was fading away.

They began their ascent into the hills. Soon, the city lay spread out below them. The source of the fire was clearly visible now. As Selma had said, it was probably a Syrian store. He dropped Selma off at the foot of the track that climbed towards the terraced rows of shanties overlooking the city. The red earth was deeply rutted and she stumbled and swayed as she made her way up the slope. He watched until she disappeared.

Chapter Ten

On his way back, he stopped at the belvedere, from where one had an uninterrupted view of the town and the harbour. On the far side of the park he could just make out through the trees the gabled roof of the old St Pierre mansion, generally regarded as one of the jewels of the city's colonial architecture. Some years before it had passed quietly out of the family's hands and become the property of the Ministry of External Affairs. It was a sale which, although not exactly compulsory, it would have been unwise to resist. His father had understood this and bowed to the inevitable. Now the green, red and yellow flag of the Cuyamese Republic flew from its much-admired gabled roof and, by day and by night, armed sentries guarded its ornate iron gates.

Truth to tell, his father must have been secretly relieved at the turn of events. The upkeep of the property had become something of a burden. In fact, the house had been falling into discreet dilapidation. The wrought-iron balconies ornamenting the upper reaches of its façade were rusting away; the roof tiles imported from France were crumbling; beneath their layers of varnish the floorboards were rotting; the paintwork was peeling; there were yellow patches on the ceilings of the lesser used rooms where the rain had soaked through; a smell of damp haunted the corridors.

The last link with that house had been broken some months ago by his mother's death. Over the years Stephanie St Pierre had made the glories of the family into which she had married her own. She treasured every relic, was acquainted with every available detail of the family history. Those who had come to the house for the first time would invariably be given a guided tour of its splendours. She led them up creaking flights of stairs to the spacious nursery near the top of the house where they were made to inspect ageing rocking horses, quaintly decorated cradles, collections of toy soldiers in the battle-dresses of Napoleonic times, daintily ornamented music boxes. She took them to the library and exhibited the mouldering collection of leather-bound books locked away behind glass-doored book-cases: books which when handled threatened to fall apart and left brown stains on the palms and fingers.

She showed them the gilt-framed canvasses, murky with varnish, executed by one of the clan's eccentrics who had lived many years in Paris and studied art. 'The family regarded him as one of their black sheep,' she explained, 'because he led a very wild, very bohemian life in Paris. He used to correspond with Monsieur Eugène Delacroix.' She puckered her lids. 'You know about Eugène Delacroix, the famous artist? Monsieur Delacroix seemed to think that he had some talent.' She drew their attention to faded Oriental rugs and to brass-studded sea-chests. She led them out into the garden to the pond covered with lilies where a kneeling Narcissus gazed at his watery reflection; and, beyond the pond, along paths slippery with moss, to the vine-embowered 'summer house' with its cupola roof crowned by a bronze Cupid aiming an arrow at the sky. Every object had its story and its associations. 'Here the young people would do their wooing,' she said as she led the way into the summer house 'At twilight the garden would be scented with jasmine. Now the roof leaks and it's all falling down. Nobody sits out here any more.'

And always, there was the solemn gathering about the portrait of Eugene St Pierre. She would narrate his story, telling of his flight from Haiti at the time of the slave rebellion there in the closing years of the eighteenth century. Almost as if she herself had been a witness of these tribulations, she would describe how, with his wife and infant son, he had arrived in Cuyama virtually without a penny to his name and with only the clothes on his back; how through the sheer weight of his ambition and his persistence he had secured for himself the managership of an indigo plantation; and how, in the space of a few years, he had prospered to the point where he was able to buy the estate from its bankrupt owner and himself become a landed proprietor. She would bring out the album of his engravings – commissioned as his memorial. The visitor saw panoramic views of the St Pierre estates; saw Eugene on horseback being saluted by his slaves; saw him on his barge being rowed upstream by slaves with shining muscles; saw him at ease in a hammock, smoking a long-stemmed pipe, with his mulatto handmaids waiting in attendance.

She would describe how the campaign to abolish slavery had roused him to fury and how, in the end, the news of its success had killed him. Occasionally, she would show copies of the letters – torrents of abuse – which he had written to William Wilberforce. 'And you know,' she might say, lightly touching the sleeve of her listener, 'I wonder if being a slave was really as bad as it is made out today. I wonder if those people (she never talked of Negroes – always they were 'those people') ... I wonder if those people are really any happier or better off now than they were then.' Her husband would try to curb these wilder aspects of her historical meditations – but without a great deal of success.

When he broke the news to her about the impending sale of the house, she refused to believe him. When she was finally made to understand that it was not a joke, she collapsed on the floor and sobbed. Aubrey had been an accidental witness of that scene. They had moved to a modishly modern house in a distant, modishly modern suburb established on lands reclaimed from the coastal swamp. Within three years of their removal, his father had died. He collapsed in his office one afternoon and was dead on arrival at the hospital. Stephanie reacted calmly to the news. She sent a telegram to her son in England, a bald statement of the fact. 'Father Died Today.' Aubrey considered it his duty to return. 'What's the point of that?' she responded over the crackling telephone line. 'What good will your coming home do? I can bury him without your help.'

Outwardly calm as she was, Charles's death was for Stephanie the final betrayal. Whatever remaining illusions she may have cherished died with him, were buried with him. Just as he had done next to nothing to prepare her for the change that was to sweep over their lives – and even afterwards had tried to play down its significance, to laugh it away – so he had done next to nothing to prepare her for his death. She was like a pampered household pet released into the wild without warning and asked to fend for itself.

It had never seriously occurred to her that she might have to live her life without him. One moment there he was, a warm, breathing body lying beside her; the next, he was snatched away from her, never to return. Just like that. Not a word of advice. Not a word of farewell. It defied comprehension. To her, so many things had been inconceivable – until they had actually happened. She was being forced to learn too many harsh lessons too late in life. The certainties on which she had been reared had proved to be no certainties at all, only a succession of empty dreams masquerading as reality. Now Aubrey had succeeded her with *his* certainties. Weren't those too as surely doomed as hers had been?

The new house, despite its faultless modernity, despite all its concessions to ease and comfort, despite all the admiration it elicited, remained for her a mere shell: a mausoleum inappropriately stocked with the furniture of another century. On the salty soil reclaimed from the virgin swamp she had tried to create a garden. The trees she had planted soon yellowed, withered and died. Still, being a creature of habit, she did her best to keep up appearances. She dressed, as always, with care, fastidiously powdered, scented and coiffured. She read what foreign magazines she could lay her hands on and kept up with the latest exhibitions and plays running in London and New York. Now and then she entertained a few friends, seeking to do so as elegantly as the circumstances permitted. She did what she could, but without conviction.

Yet, there were times when her self-control would fray. It was then, making use of the person nearest to hand, she would unburden herself to her daughter-in-law. 'Never believe everything a man tells you,' she said. 'Never take anything for granted. The world is built on quicksand. It will drown you unless you take care and know what you're doing. Don't let yourself be fooled as I was fooled.' As Dina listened to the son, so she listened to the mother.

Even the suburb, created in such a burst of optimism twenty years before, was decaying. Many of the houses, vacated in haste by their panic-stricken owners who had fled abroad, were falling into ruin, battered by sun and rain. Squatters, migrating from the countryside and the overcrowded, red-earthed hills encircling Charlestown, had invaded several of these properties. No one made any attempt to evict them. Potholes cratered the lanes and grass sprouted between the blocks of paving. The roundabouts which in earlier days had been adorned with beds of flowers were tangles of weeds. Broken streetlights were not repaired and drifts of litter piled up in the gutters. At night, lying awake, Stephanie would listen to the howls of the packs of stray dogs – pets abandoned to the wilderness by their owners – foraging along the lanes, fighting over the scraps.

'You ought to move out of here,' Aubrey said. 'Find a place in town. Or come and live with us.'

'I've done my moving,' she replied. Her gaze swept over the blighted remnants of the garden she had tried to make. 'When I'm gone, you can do with this place as you like. It's unhallowed ground. I don't really care what happens to it and I don't suppose you do either. You can do what you like with the furniture. Sell it. Or give it all away to those people over there.' She tilted her head towards a nearby house which had been taken over by squatters who had planted maize on what had been a lawn. 'Let them use it for firewood or whatever.'

'You pity yourself too much, Mother. It's not healthy.'

'So,' she said, smiling back at him, 'you would deny me even pity for myself. You would have even that taken away from me.'

To which accusation he had made no answer.

Like his father, she had died without warning, carried off in her sleep. She had been buried one rainy afternoon beside her husband in the plot reserved for the St Pierres in the Charlestown cemetery.

*

Once, on impulse, he took Dina to the old place. But the sentries posted at the gate would not let them enter. They gazed at it through a gap in the hedge. Many alterations and innovations had been carried out. The rusting balconies of wrought-iron had been removed. Metal awnings painted a luminous green had replaced the fretted wooden eaves fring-ing the verandas. From the windows protruded clattering, dripping air-conditioners. The fruit trees had been cut down. Beyond, covering the spot where Narcissus had once gazed at his reflection in the pond and the site previously occupied by the 'summer house', a brick addition had been built.

'Perhaps it's just as well they won't let us in,' he said as they went away.

*

'It was as if something snapped when we moved out of the old house,' Aubrey had said to her. 'Some vital link was broken. It's not at all easy to describe. The world seemed to become a much more uncertain and dangerous place. Nothing was ever the same after that. I remember our last

139

morning very clearly. We were gathered on the front veranda like a group of refugees, watching the remaining bits
and pieces of furniture being taken away. It was not in the
least like a straightforward transference from one house to
another. It was as though the bailiffs had come in, as
though we were being dispossessed and driven away.

'At a certain level, that was indeed the case. We were
leaving that big, old house not because we wanted to but
because we had to. Our little role in history had been
played out. The St Pierres – former owners of slaves and
vast estates – were *finished* and there was nothing that
could be done about it. My mother was crying – she had
been crying for months – and Father was trying his best to
comfort her. Despite the brave, commonsense interpretation he put on the affair, I think even he understood on
that final morning the enormity of what was happening to
us. He too had come to understand that the St Pierres had
reached the end of the road. I remember my mother
saying, "What will happen to this lovely garden now? Who
will care for it? Who will recall the things that have happened in it?"

'And I heard myself muttering, "Who cares what happens to it? It no longer belongs to us, does it?"

'It was a completely unpremeditated remark. The words
formed themselves, spoke themselves. My mother turned
and looked at me. Father spun round and slapped me.
Slapped me very hard. I can still feel the sting of that blow
on my cheek.'

He rubbed the spot, smiling at the woman who, a few
weeks before, had become his wife.

'I was seventeen years old at the time. Until then, I had
never seriously questioned anything. There was not the
smallest trace of the rebel in me. You might say I was the
little Lord Fauntleroy my mother had always wanted me to
be. I was the boy she had dressed up in a sailor suit with
brass buttons. There was a photograph of me dressed up

like that. It used to hang in the nursery. I don't know what's become of it.

'Until that moment I had never tried to see us as others must see us. I had never given "those people" – as Mother called them – a thought. They were just out there, leading their invisible lives somewhere beyond our bushy hedge. To me, they were utterly alien and mysterious, an altogether different species of animal. I had never made any connection between myself and them.

'I knew them as servants who came to our house to cook and iron and sweep and polish. They called me "Master Aubrey" because my mother insisted that they should do so. It seemed the most natural thing in the world that I should be addressed as "Master" by women old enough to be grandmothers.'

The dark pools of his eyes dilated in wry disbelief. As he talked, he played with his wispy beard. She listened intently, not interrupting, watching him with a distant curiosity: one stranger listening to the story of another stranger.

'There was a boy of roughly my own age, Desmond, the son of the woman who came in two or three times a week to do the washing and ironing. I used to play with Desmond a fair amount. Outdoors, it goes without saying. I could only play outdoor games with Desmond because he was not permitted beyond the corridor leading from the kitchen. Again, that restriction on our activities didn't strike me as peculiar. It was unthinkable as much for me as for my mother that he should have any further privileges. Desmond in our drawing-room – unimaginable!

'With Desmond I was the perfect autocrat. He was merely a convenient sort of animal who answered a particular set of needs. I never consulted his feelings or preferences. They were not of the slightest concern to me. Desmond played what I wanted to play, when I wanted to play, and for just as long as I wanted to play. During the hours he spent with me, he was not allowed to have either a life or a will of his own.

141

He was there to be summoned and discarded at the click of a finger. There were times when Desmond didn't want to do anything, when all he seemed to want to do was sit in some patch of shade in the garden and day-dream. He was a strangely lethargic sort of boy, a consequence, I now suspect, of under-nourishment.

'If Desmond showed any kind of reluctance to join in the silly games I proposed, I would become angry and threaten him with banishment from our garden. Usually, his mother intervened. "Desmond," she would shout at him, "you must do as Master Aubrey tell you to do. This is his house, not yours. If you don't do as he tell you, I'll skin you alive." And Desmond would obey. Sourly, grimacing as though on the verge of tears, he would rise to his feet and stand respectfully before me, awaiting my commands. It torments me to think of it now.

'When I was called in to lunch or dinner, I would leave bare-footed, dusty Desmond with his fraying khaki short-pants sitting out on the back steps. When we had finished eating, he would be given a scrap or two of our leftovers, served up to him on a chipped enamel plate you'd think twice about offering to a dog. Those were probably the only times in the week when Desmond saw meat. I used to watch him eat, fascinated by his gulping greed. He ate with a self-absorbed, intense concentration, chewing hard and noisily, licking his greasy fingers as though he were in half a mind to gulp them down too, scouring the plate clean with his tongue. It was a compelling performance. Desmond was expected to be grateful – he wasn't on the payroll. The food we gave him was considered a wonderful act of charity.

'I wonder what used to go through that mind of his. How he must have resented and hated me – both him and his mother who would look on silently while I ordered about her son. It must have violated every maternal instinct in her. Yet, neither she nor Desmond ever openly rebelled. They absorbed their punishment without complaint. How else would Desmond have obtained those plates of food? Where else would his mother have found another job with a salary so decent? For, by the standards of her class, my mother was a good employer. She paid those who worked for her generous wages, bought them medicines when they fell ill, gave them presents at Christmas. It was not unknown for her to sit down in the maid's room and share a cup of tea. Oh yes, she did all the correct things. She did everything that was expected of her and more. She would have been genuinely horrified if anyone had reproached her with being callous. She would've had no idea what they were talking about.

'When I was eleven or twelve, I was forbidden from playing even outdoor games with Desmond. He would still accompany his mother to the house, sitting out patiently on the back steps near the kitchen while she did the washing and the ironing. But from then on Desmond and I had nothing to do with each other. I stopped being aware of his existence. Desmond, no doubt, must have had no regrets. Now he could relax without fear of disturbance in the shade and day-dream as much as he liked – and still have his enamel plate filled with our left-overs. Our separation, like everything else, had seemed natural enough to me. I questioned nothing. I let everything happen. Some years ago – not long, in fact, after my return from England, I suddenly remembered Desmond and tried to find out what had become of him. My attempt was a failure. My mother couldn't even recall his surname. I'm not sure what I would have done if I'd found him. Apologise? Fall on my knees like a penitent before him? I don't know. If you were Desmond, wouldn't you have hated me?'

'If *I* were Desmond . . .' she murmured. 'Yes, I suppose if I had been Desmond I would have hated you. But it's possible the real Desmond never hated you. Or, at least, wouldn't have known that he ought to hate you. Maybe he didn't regard it as strange or unjust that he was as he was and you were as you were.'

'In time he would have learned to hate – just as I, in time, have struggled to understand and atone. Today he probably marches with the mob, thirsting for blood. Can we blame him for that?'

She shook her head, gazing abstractedly at him.

'As I was saying,' he went on,' something snapped when we were forced out of that old house. Standing there on the veranda that morning with my mother weeping and that slap from my father burning on my cheek, I had a vision of sorts. I saw our isolation, our ignorance, our unfounded arrogance. What was there to be proud of in our dismal record? What was there to be mourned? For the first time I saw the St Pierres as others must have seen us. I saw the unreality – the artificiality – of our lives. We were worse than refugees. We were corpses, washed up and stranded by the tides of history.

'My father had understood what the coming of Independence might mean for a family like us. He grasped the fact that he would have to make new alliances and new friendships in unlikely quarters. My mother appreciated none of this. She could not understand why my father had begun to invite so many black men into our drawing-room. "Take a good look around you," I once heard him say to her. "Observe the colours of the flags you see flying from the public buildings. We're citizens of the Republic of Cuyama now. The slaves are the rulers. Even the St Pierres have to face facts. We must become new people."

'I had remained splendidly aloof from the ferment caused by the coming of Independence. I was contemptuous of the excitement it generated among the boys at school. You must remember what the atmosphere was like at the time – all those marches and rallies, all those impromptu gatherings at street corners, all those random acts of violence. Living in the timeless bubble created by my mother, it had seemed that nothing could really ever touch us. But there we were, all the same, gathered on the veranda, watching our possessions being taken out of the house and dumped on the tray of a lorry.

'I started to read. I discovered Karl Marx and began to call myself a Marxist. To my mother I'd say the most hurtful and outrageous things. The St Pierres, I'd tell her, were bloodsuckers and parasites. We deserved whatever we had coming to us. My father laughed it off, telling her it was a phase all adolescents went through. Of course, I was at that age when one enjoys creating an effect. Nevertheless, my fervour wasn't all spurious. I was seeing the world with new eyes and I was genuinely intoxicated.

'It had always been taken for granted that I would follow in my father's footsteps, become a solicitor like him. My future was so pre-destined that it had never even been discussed. I chose my eighteenth birthday to announce, so to speak, my abdication. My life, I declared, would be conse-crated to nobler aims than money-making. There was little they could do – the fight had gone out of them. Father was already showing the first symptoms of the disease that was soon to kill him and Mother was punch-drunk. At that moment, I felt sorry for them. My mind, though, was made up. "With luck," my father remarked on the day of my departure, "you'll come to your senses one of these days."'

Aubrey spread his arms wide, smiling at her. 'Here I am, still not restored to my senses.'

*

Making one of his routine visits since his mother's death to the house in that decaying suburb reclaimed from the coastal swamp, Aubrey discovered that it had been occupied by a family of squatters. Lines of dripping washing were laid out across the garden. Here and there window-panes had been broken and patched with cardboard. A woman, a naked child propped on her hip, came up to take a look at him as he sat hunched over the steering-wheel of the Morris Minor.

'You want something, Mister?' she asked.

He shook his head. 'No,' he replied. 'I don't want anything. I was just ...' The sentence remained unfinished. He
drove away, determined never to go back.

He told Dina what had happened.

'I don't suppose your mother would have minded,' she
said. 'She never cared for that place.'

'It's strange nevertheless.'

'What is strange?'

'To know that it's all ended. The saga of the St Pierres, I
mean.'

'Isn't that what you wanted?'

'Yes. But I somehow never imagined that it would be like
that.'

'Like what?'

'I never imagined the final act would be so casual, so
matter-of-fact ... so grotesquely simple. One expects more
from a historic moment.' He smiled joylessly at her.

'And all you had,' she said, 'was a squatter woman hanging out washing and a naked child. I agree with you. Life
should reach its climaxes with more of a flourish.'

Telling no one, he performed another of his rites of
renunciation: he handed over to the National Museum of
Cuyama – one of those institutions that existed more in
name than in fact – the collection of engravings his mother
used to exhibit so proudly to visitors to the old house. 'I
consider it my duty to do this,' he wrote to the Minister
concerned. 'It seems proper and just that this unique historical record should become the property of the people of
Cuyama.'

A frenzied Beatrice arrived at the bookshop one morning.

'What's this nonsense I've been hearing?' she asked.

'What nonsense?' Aubrey, who was sitting at his desk,
gazed up calmly at her.

'Don't pretend. You know perfectly well what I'm talking
about – that album of engravings. Believe me, there's
nothing that goes on in this place which I don't hear about.'

'What about them?' he remained unmoved by her agitation.

She raised her already loud voice. 'Is it true that you handed them over to the so-called National Museum? Is it possible that you – even you! – could have done something so foolish?' She pounded the desk with her fist.

'I fail to see what business it is of yours.'

'You fail to see, do you?' She leaned across the desk, bringing her face close to his. 'Your trouble is that you fail to see every goddamned thing.' She pounded the desk again, tossing back her head. Her fleshy neck glistened with sweat. The smell of her perfume swirled about him. Dina, attracted by the commotion, came and stood in the curtained doorway. Beatrice strode up and down the shop, mouthing inaudible imprecations at the ceiling. Aubrey was immune to his first cousin's excitability. Her greed, that never-ending quest for what she described as security, fascinated him. Her ostentatious 'realism' had become a disease. She catapulted herself back to the desk. 'Do you have any idea of the worth of that collection?'

'Their financial value is of no interest to me.'

'Thousands of dollars. You washed thousands of dollars down the drain. Do you understand that? My friend in New York . . .'

'I'm not interested in your friend in New York. That collection belongs to the people of Cuyama and to no one else.'

She snorted, laughing in his face. 'You might believe you've given them to the people of Cuyama. But what do you think the Minister plans to do with your gift?'

Aubrey's self-assurance wavered.

'I'll put you out of your misery. I'll tell you what he plans to do with your wonderful bequest to the nation.' Her voice rose to a shriek. 'He plans to sell them. To my New York friend who doesn't interest you. The Minister isn't stupid like you. He knows what that collection is worth on the open market.'

He gazed fixedly at her. Her scented face grew indistinct.

'My noble cousin! You'd like to believe I'm lying, wouldn't you? That man would sell his grandmother if the price was right. He would sell the Cuyamese people – your dear Cuyamese people – right back into slavery if the offer was right. He doesn't lose sleep over principles.' She switched her attention to Dina. 'What has your husband got inside that head of his? What? What?' Close to angry tears, she was sweating even more profusely.

Aubrey cradled his head in his hands. 'I won't let him get away with it.'

Beatrice was highly entertained by that flicker of defiance. 'And how will you set about doing that? They'd squash you like they'd squash a mosquito.' She jabbed her thumb on the desk in emphatic mimicry. She paused, gathering breath. 'If nothing has happened to you yet, that's only because I've taken the trouble to put in a word for you here and there. If it wasn't for the little influence Ralph and I have in certain quarters, you wouldn't be here now writing all those stupid letters protesting about this and that to the foreign press.'

Aubrey winced. 'How altruistic you are.' But his misery showed through the feeble attempt at raillery. She was quite right, of course. What could he do? He stared down at his sandalled feet. Here he was, a grown man, indulging himself in boy-scout notions of honour and fair play in a jungle teeming with predators. A lumbering weariness swept over him.

That evening, as he sat out with Dina on the dark veranda, he said: 'I've been very stupid.'

'What is done is done,' she murmured back. 'I wouldn't worry about it now.'

'It never occurred to me that they could be so breath-takingly cynical,' he said. All the same, it was not about the engravings he wanted to talk. He wanted to talk about himself, but he didn't know how to begin.

'No,' she said. 'I don't suppose it ever did occur to you.'

A small breeze stirred the leaves of the orange-tree; the frogs croaked with frenzied energy.

'I wonder what goes on inside those heads of theirs,' he said. 'Why is it that they aren't driven mad by all their lies, all their betrayals?'

'They don't have to be driven mad. They are mad. We're all cracked. You, me, Beatie, the Minister. Cuyama is one big lunatic asylum.'

'Do you really believe that?'

'I don't know. It's just an opinion.' She gestured irritably.

'I don't know either what I really believe. Not any more.'

She glanced towards him, taken aback by the disclosure.

'My life has been a series of futile gestures,' he went on. 'An elaborate hoax – of which I myself have been the chief victim. Day after day I've sat in that bookshop telling myself lies, believing that I was doing something, making a contribution, by simply being there. But what kind of contribution was I making? What was I actually doing? It was a form of egoism, nothing more.' The rounded pools of his eyes were luminous in the darkness. 'We go abroad and we see how other people live. We study at their universities, we read their books, we admire their paintings and their fine buildings, we walk in their parks. Then we return home and discover that, in terms of what we've experienced, we're barely human. We discover that we've done nothing worthy of interest, don't know how to do anything and, perhaps, don't even want to do anything. And you say, "I'll help to change all this. The degeneracy I see around me is merely a distortion. It's the result of colonialism, slavery, economic exploitation – what have you". You become, as Beatrice would say, a big-time intellectual – though all that is meant is that you try to develop rational responses to your environment. But then you discover that men are not educable. Or, at least, not automatically so. What urge was it that made men living on the banks of the Tigris and Euphrates and Nile take to the disciplines of settled agriculture? What made them build cities and study the stars and develop the art of writing? What they were doing was discovering the seeds of their humanity. They were making the remarkable discovery that they were men. In Cuyama we haven't made that discovery. Because the seeds of our humanity lie unfertilised, we remain ineducable. We do not know we are men. That is why we will remain as we are – unreflecting creatures of appetite. In a frenzy of self-regard I sat day after day in my bookshop, explaining away my failures, refusing to recognise my futility.'

She did not attempt a denial.

*

He sat on the parapet of the belvedere. Below him, a litter-hazed slope fell away to a colony of shanties. The shouts of children floated in the air, rising up from the welter of corrugated-iron roofs spreading out from the base of the cliff face. Dogs barked. Somewhere a cock crowed and another answered. Black-winged scavenger birds circled slowly against the cloudless sky. He sat on the parapet, fanned by a light wind, listening to the noises of man and beast, and watched the fire spread its brown haze over the city.

Chapter Eleven

They drove westward out of Charlestown, moving through decaying streets and avenues, the ageing taxi rattling over the potholes. Litter clogged the gutters, filmed the waste places. Gangs of schoolchildren snaked along the dusty verges. Matted-haired young men stared from under the eaves of rumshops and foodstalls. Everywhere he saw the shells of burnt-out buildings. He saw the foundations of vanished houses, archways leading nowhere. He gazed down alleys lined with shanties. Fires smouldered in the gullies.

Dina, her face averted, was silent. In this chaos she lived. Out of this chaos she had been formed. It was not easy to comprehend.

Alex looked at her, sitting across the seat from him.

He said: 'I didn't know there had been a civil war.'

'There hasn't.' She laughed, turning towards him.

'Why then all these ruins?'

'I don't know,' she said. 'I'm not a philosopher. When you live here, you cease to notice. You accept. You become accustomed. I thought you'd be more case-hardened. You must have seen so much in your travels.'

'I get the impression you don't like me,' he said.

'Why should I like you?' She had put on her dark glasses again.

Eventually, they came in sight of the sea. They followed the curve of the bay. The town was petering out, the road narrowing. On the right, the land rose steeply up to the hills; on the left the sea was grey and glassy. Fishing boats were drawn up on a crescent of pebbly beach. Nets, stretched out

151

on tall poles, were drying in the sun. A man slept in the shade of a coconut tree. He could make out the protuberance of a misty headland in the distance.

She pointed. 'The fort's at the tip of that,' she said.

He said, 'Ah ...'

She smiled. 'You're angry with me. I didn't mean to be rude.'

'I'm not angry with you. How could I be? You've sacrificed your time to show me the sights.'

'I've told you – it's no sacrifice. I'm a lady of leisure.' She continued to smile at him.

The shoreline became fringed with mangrove. Dark water gleamed amid the lattice-work of roots.

They were approaching a stall offering for sale tiny heaps of sun-baked fruit.

'We ought to get some oranges,' she said. 'There won't be anything up at the fort.'

She told the driver to stop. He watched her negotiate with the woman in charge, a woman as old and wrinkled as the fruit she was selling, taking shelter from the sun under a tattered panama hat. Flies circled round the stall. The driver, breathing heavily, fanned himself with a newspaper. His fat neck glistened with sweat. Dina, choosing the oranges with care, was taking her time. Alex breathed in the mingled odours of sea and swamp. He stared at Dina, picking up and putting down oranges. At last it was done. Alex leaned over and opened the door for her.

'Success?'

'Success.'

They started off. Dina cradled the oranges on her lap.

'These oranges aren't like the ones you get in London,' she said. 'But they can be very sweet.' She held up one for his inspection: a small, greenish-yellow object.

Alex took the orange from her and examined it attentively.

'I'd imagine it's a wild, undomesticated strain,' she said.

'Just like everything else in Cuyama. Why don't you try one?' She asked the driver if he had a penknife.

The driver did indeed have a penknife. She peeled the orange, sliced it in two and passed it to him. She wiped the blade of the penknife and returned it to the driver.

Alex sucked experimentally at the orange.

'Excellent,' he said. 'Wild, undomesticated strains have their own distinct charms.' He laughed. 'Often far superior to tame, cultivated ones.' He lapped the dribbling juice off his fingers.

They were now not much more than a mile away from the headland, a green arm lying on the grey mirror of the sea. On its far tip he could see winding, crenellated walls. They emphasised the virgin desolation of this mangrove-fringed coast.

'Tell me about the fort.' Alex licked his sticky fingers.

'Most of what you see dates from the beginning of the eighteenth century. But, before that, the Spanish had built some sort of watch-tower up there and, later on, the Dutch added to it. But what you see now is nearly all British. Do you know anything at all about the history of Cuyama?'

'Very little.'

'Once upon a time we were regarded as a valuable prize.'

'What went wrong?'

'The wild, undomesticated strains triumphed, I suppose.' She smiled at him. 'Aubrey's the expert. His family played quite a role in the history of Cuyama.'

'And what about your family?' he asked lightly.

'My family?' She became sombre, staring out across the water. 'I don't really know. Their deeds have not been recorded. On my father's side they worked on the sugar estates. On my mother's they were small shopkeepers. They described themselves as Portuguese.'

'I know a little bit about the St Pierres,' he said. 'Aubrey used to tell me about them.'

'I expect he would have,' she remarked dully.

153

'A colourful crew by all accounts.'

'Very colourful.'

He gazed at the headland, anchored in the mirror-like sea. They left the main road, jolting on to a rutted track. Dust billowed in their wake. They rolled up the windows. A scrubby wilderness enclosed the track. The leaves of the trees and bushes were powdered white. Above them was a strip of cloudless sky. Alex studied the vegetation. Palms rose here and there like neat green fountains. The spindly trunks of the trees were wreathed with creepers. Lianas trailed from high branches. He heard echoing, croaking noises that may have been the calls of birds. The tangled gloom stretched as far as the eye could see. Sealed in by the featureless strip of blue sky, the strangely lifeless jungle, the clouds of dust raised by the car, it was as if they had been sucked out of familiar time and place; cast adrift in the dead eye of nothingness. It was odd to recall that they had left Charlestown barely an hour ago; odd to think that not far away was the sea. The track climbed steadily. Dina held a handkerchief to her nose.

'Nearly there,' she said.

The track flattened; the jungle receded; the fort came into view. A Cuyamese flag flapped from its central tower. The driver halted in the shade of a tree. A brisk wind scoured the headland. Before them rose the crumbling walls encircling the sea-facing front of the fort. Rusting cannon poked their muzzles through the crenellations. Various outbuildings were scattered about. Most of these were roofless.

'I did tell you there wasn't a great deal,' she said, her voice abducted by the wind, her hands pressed down against the front of her dress to protect it from the assaults of the buffeting gusts. The driver, hands in pockets, trailed behind them, looking vacantly about him. It was the most modest of fortifications. They walked through windswept grass to the notice-board put up by the Cuyamese Ministry of Education and Culture. This provided a summary of the fort's history. It more or less repeated what Dina had told him. There was no one else about. Butterflies danced among the grasses. They strolled slowly in the sunshine, inspecting the buildings, peering through rusting iron grilles at dark interiors out of which rose the smells of long abandonment.

'Doesn't anyone ever come here?' he asked.

'Hardly,' she said. 'You see what the road's like. Once, a long time ago, I came here with my family to have a picnic.' She blinked into the glare. 'But it's a very, very faint memory. I must have been extremely young.'

'And you haven't been here since?'

She shook her head. The wind whipped at her hair. She clutched at the skirt of her dress. The driver had returned to the car. He watched them sleepily.

'Come,' she said, 'let's have a look at the view.'

They made their way to the ramparts. In both directions the green of the mangrove-fringed shoreline faded away into a milky haze. They could see the white buildings of Charlestown and the grey sparkle of the roadstead where a few ships lay at anchor. She pointed out to him the spire of the cathedral and a few other landmarks. He stared at the hills with their terraced layers of shanties. Below them, the land fell steeply to the sea and the mangrove in a tangle of vegetation and rocky outcrops. They stood without speaking at the ramparts, considering the view, that disturbing desolation of city and wilderness, sky and water. The wind whipped and eddied about them. She assumed her peculiar, inward-looking expression which made her seem so remote, so detached, from her surroundings.

'Up here,' she said, 'you begin to get a truer idea of Cuyama.'

'Explain that to me,' he said.

'I'm not very good at explaining,' she replied. 'I mean you get a better idea of the nonsense of it all,' she went on after a while. She turned towards him, her eyes hooded against the glare. 'It's a bit like living out a hallucination. There are times, moments, when it seems so absurd, so unreal, that you

155

almost begin to doubt whether you actually exist ...' She stopped herself with a dismissive flick of her wrist. 'I can't think why I'm telling you all this nonsense. It can't possibly be of any interest to you. Your idea of the "Third World" and mine must be so impossibly different.'

'Why impossibly different?'

'You write about it – that's your job. I live in it – that's my fate. Don't you see the difference?'

'You're mocking me.'

'No,' she said, becoming sombre. 'I'm not mocking you. If I'm mocking at anything it's myself.' She ran her hands along the coping of the rampart. 'You at least have a skill you can be proud of.'

Alex frowned towards the hazy sprawl of the city. Insects whirred about them. The wind was dying down and the sea heaved with a lifeless sparkle. The shadows were creeping towards them. She moved away from him, walking along the rampart, looking out to sea. He watched her, admiring the erect, easy gait.

'When I was young,' she said, 'I used to dream of sailing away in a big, white ship.'

'Sailing away where?'

'Anywhere. To the farthest ends of the earth. I wanted to be real. I wanted to be like other people.'

'And what happened to that dream?'

'It died.'

She kept her back turned on him, her hand resting on the warm coping. He did not take his eyes off her.

She said, observing the lengthening shadows: 'Maybe we ought to be getting back.'

'Yes,' he replied, stirring himself. 'Maybe we ought to.'

She glanced at her watch. 'The taxi's going to charge us a small fortune.'

'Don't let that worry you.'

'I keep forgetting you're on expenses.' She bestowed on him one of her sourly mischievous smiles.

They walked languidly away from the rampart, she going on ahead of him.

'I could spend whole days in places like this,' he said. 'Forts are good for dreaming.'

'Even Cuyamese forts?'

'Even Cuyamese forts.'

Their voices rang through the stillness. For a moment, moving through the heat across the grass, it did suddenly seem to him that he was sharing in the sense of hallucination to which she had referred. She floated like an apparition before him, an emanation of the heat and light and stillness.

The taxi driver slept, his head thrown back over the seat, his mouth agape. The newspaper he had used to cover his face had slipped down on to his lap. Above them, the Cuyamese flag hung limp from its tower.

They returned to the city. Neither of them had much to say on the way back.

*

The boat drifted on the wide, wind-rippled water. Remotely edged with mangrove, the swamp resembled an inland sea. Beyond rose the mountains, clouds hovering about their blue summits. Alex lounged on the deck, in the full blast of the sun, drinking beer and talking to Ralph. She and Beatrice lay under the awning.

'The Interior,' Ralph was saying. 'That's where the future of Cuyama lies.' As he talked, he lazily massaged himself, now and again slapping his flesh with the flat of his palms. The sound of flesh on flesh was loud in the echoing stillness. Ralph's smooth skin glistened.

'What nonsense,' Beatrice said, going up to them. She looked at Alex. 'We all talk about the future of Cuyama being in the Interior when we all know that this place has no kind of future in any direction. It's sauve qui peut.'

Ralph laughed and rolled over on his back. He was as

silky, as torpid, as a sated beast of prey. Beatrice pummelled him with affection.

Alex crawled off to the awning. He crouched next to
Dina. She put aside the novel she was reading. He lifted up
the cover and looked at the title.

'Lawrence,' he said.

'Do you like him?'

'I hardly read at all nowadays.' The colourless water
lapped against the sides of the boat.

She stared at the sun streaking the water. Beatrice and
Ralph were giggling over some private joke. Beatrice
jumped up from beside her husband with a loud shriek of
merriment.

'I suppose,' she said, 'you have so many other things to fill
up your days with. I'm not sure what I'd do without books.'
She pulled the striped towel draped over her shoulders like a
shawl more closely about her. Her eyes assumed their
veiled, hooded expression. The water gurgled and lapped;
the boat moved gently beneath them. She folded her arms
across her knees.

'How lucky you are,' she said.

'Why am I lucky?'

'Tomorrow you'll be gone. In a couple of weeks – or less –
all this will seem like a dream.' She gestured inconsequen-
tially at the water, the hills, the mangrove. 'You'll go away,
write your articles, claim your expenses ...' She laughed.

'You too will forget all about me.'

'Naturally. I'll go on reading my books.' She stared at
him. 'Have you ever heard of the horse dance?'

He shook his head.

'The Javanese who came here brought it with them. Or so
I've been told. In the dance, the men slowly get taken over
by the spirits of various animals. Some become like monkeys
and tear apart unhusked coconuts with their teeth. Others
become tigers and bite off the heads of chickens. And some,
of course, become horses, stamping and snorting and pawing

the ground. When it's done they fall into a trance, collapsing in a kind of rigor mortis. It's very frightening. I was taken to see one when I was a child.'

'Sounds like a combination of hysteria and self-hypnosis,' he said.

'You talk like Aubrey.'

He was a little taken aback by this. 'Why – do you believe that these people really do get taken over by the spirits of animals?'

Beatrice and Ralph continued to screech with laughter.

'It's not so much that I believe it. It's that I fear the possibility.' Her eyes went lustrous with sudden laughter. 'How anxious you look! Do you fear for my sanity? It's merely a fantasy I have.'

'What's the fantasy?'

'That in a place like this we may, in some distant future, be permanently taken over, permanently possessed. Evolution in reverse, if you like. In a hundred years, we might all be stamping and pawing the ground, biting off the heads of live chickens, tearing apart unhusked coconuts with our bare teeth.'

Leaping to her feet, she went off to join Ralph and Beatrice.

Later, they moored in an inlet. They swam in a deep, dark-watered pool surrounded by the forest. Afterward, they lay on the rocks. Patches of blue sky showed through the trees. The sun fell in dusty bands across the rocks. Ralph and Beatrice disappeared: they said they were going to search for oysters.

She sat with her arms clasped about her knees which were drawn up nearly to her chin. She gazed at the black water. Picking up a pebble she tossed it into the pool and watched the widening rings of disturbance it created on the smooth surface. She turned to look at him, lying spreadeagled on the warm rock, her face gone taut with fury. 'What do you want from us?' she asked. 'Why do you come all this way merely to observe our misery, to feed on it? Why can't you and your kind leave us alone?' She tossed another pebble into the black water.

Raising himself, he stared at her. 'Do you hate me so much?' he asked.

'Hate you?' Calming herself, she appeared to consider the question. 'No,' she said at last. 'I don't hate you. I envy you. I wish that I too could be a bird of passage. I wish that I too could let it all fade away behind me, could fly away in a big, shining machine. I don't hate you. I hate myself. I hate what I am.'

Somewhere, far away among the lattice of mangrove, they could hear Beatrice's echoing laughter.

'I would like to be a real human being,' she said. 'Nothing extraordinary. Just real. I want to stop being afraid that I might turn into an animal.' She tossed a third pebble into the water.

'You look real enough to me,' he said.

'Appearances can be deceptive,' she replied.

He smiled at her.

'I only look human,' she added. 'We all only look human.'

She hugged herself, drawing in her knees as if she were cold. 'Are there English people called Mallingham?'

'There may be. Why do you ask?'

'I wonder what they'd make of me.' She laughed. 'I asked because it was the name my grandfather took when he changed his religion and became a convert to Christianity. I grew up, you know, without allegiance to anything. I'm nothing but a mongrelised ghost of a human being living in a mongrelised ghost of a country. There's nothing holding me together. Every day I have to re-invent myself.' Rising, she moved to the edge of the rock, contemplating her reflection in the black water. The sun was sinking. In the fading light, her attitude was one of repose. He remained where he was. The sun was golden on the hills; the swamp was a restless sparkle. Through the stillness came a splash of oars. Beat-

160

rice and Ralph were returning from their oyster-hunting expedition.

She said, 'I only tell you these things because you're a bird of passage.' She smiled at him without rancour. 'Do you understand even a little of what I'm trying to say?'

'Only a little.'

Beatrice and Ralph appeared at the mouth of the creek.

'Oysters galore,' Beatrice shouted, holding up a jute bag.

As the sun set, they watched the flocks of birds returning to their roosts in the mangrove.

*

Alex re-read the hastily scrawled sentences sloping across the page. Certain expressions stood out: 'struggle'; 'liberation'; 'culture'; 'national identity'.

There floated before him the bored, ironic face of the Minister, flashy in his colourful bush shirt, whom he had interviewed earlier that afternoon.

A pointless meeting.

He recalled the hot streets through which he had walked, the long wait in the ante-room in which ceiling fans stirred the heavy air, the uncommunicative secretaries dozing over typewriters. For years he had been fed generalities not worth wasting ink on. More than ever he moved like a somnambulist across the face of the planet. Once, there had been passion in his work. Now, there was only the habit of travel laid like a curse upon him.

Tossing aside the pen, he closed his eyes. On the wall behind him, the ageing air-conditioner roared and rattled, offering merely a notional relief from the day's heat. The melting stumps of the candles he had had to light littered the room. He listened to the sounds of the traffic and the murmurs of the crowd permanently assembled outside the hotel.

Once, there had been passion in his work. Once, he had believed that all men could be redeemed.

Hauling himself up, he went out to the little balcony

overlooking the road. Dust swirled in golden clouds over the park. He leaned on the balcony railing, watching the tropical twilight thicken, watching the bats wheel out from the roof-tops and trees, watching the coconut sellers illumine their carts with flambeaux.

'Honky!' Someone was shouting at him from the road.

He went back inside. A well-aimed bottle shattered against the balcony railing. He looked at his notes.

He ripped out the pages across which he had written and flung them into the wastepaper basket. After all, it was of no consequence; it had only been a stop-over. Maybe one day, if he felt in the mood, he might write a paragraph or two about it. He started to pack.

*

Early the following morning Aubrey drove Alex out to the airport, traversing again the desolation of plain and field and forest.

'It's a pity your stay was so short,' Aubrey said.

Alex, not answering, let his gaze drift over the wide, wasted land.

'When is the article likely to be published?' Aubrey asked.

'I couldn't be sure. That's up to my editor.' He paused. 'It won't be a very long piece, you know.' Alex avoided looking at him, contemplating the rolling vistas of sugar-cane, the straggling settlement of wooden houses and huts bordering the road on one side. The mongrels snarled and leapt at the wheels of the car. He thought of Dina, standing on the veranda, wrapped in a flowered dressing-gown, waving goodbye in the cool morning. He recalled her limp hand resting briefly in his own, exactly as it had done on the afternoon of his arrival: already it was as though he were evoking some faint, fantastic memory.

'Whatever its length, don't forget to send me a copy.'

'I won't forget.'

For some time neither spoke. They left the cane-land

behind them, the road unwinding itself between walls of jungle.

Aubrey turned and looked at him. 'It's all pretty hopeless, isn't it? Not worth wasting ink on.'

'What is?'

'Us. This place.' Aubrey lifted a hand off the steering wheel, gesturing at the wilderness; but his voice was tired and without emphasis. 'Dina's right, you know. Having or not having a Constitution makes not a jot of difference to the likes of us. In your writing pay heed to her, not me. I deal only in pieties.'

'You exaggerate ...'

'You know I don't. The facts speak for themselves. They shout at us from the leaves of the trees, the stones, the hills. And they all have the same tale to tell.'

They went past the charcoal-burner's clearing. Grey wisps of smoke eddied up from the charred earth.

'The Aurora will die its fated death. Not that I'll actually close it down. Even now I lack the courage to perform that simple act!' Aubrey laughed. 'It will merely die of its own accord, succumb to the universal laws of inanity. With every day that goes by it seems more and more like a mirage. In due course it will fade away, vanish without a trace into the Cuyamese emptiness. In time, it will be as if it had never been.'

Across a vista of cleared land, the control tower of the airport came into view.

'What will you do then?'

'I don't know. What is there left to do? Maybe Dina and I will go off into the Interior. Maybe I'll begin to write that book about the Bush Folk.'

'A missionary told me they're leaving the jungle, that there're only old folk and children left in the villages.'

Aubrey laughed again. 'Quite true. It was only another pious fantasy. I suppose all we can do is await *our* fated dissolution. It will be as if we too had never existed. Look! There's your plane.'

The giant aircraft, its fuselage flashing golden in the sunlight, gleamed on a distant runway.

Five minutes later Aubrey eased the Morris Minor into the car park. He carried the suitcase into the echoing departure hall, walking briskly to the check-in counter. Soldiers lounged against the unpainted walls, rifles aslant on their shoulders.

The two men embraced.

'Who knows when – or if – we shall meet again?' Aubrey's saddened eyes played over his friend's face.

'Of course we will.' Alex detached himself from the embrace. 'Of course we will – why shouldn't we?' He smiled, punched him playfully in the stomach and, their final cries of farewell drowned by the public address, walked quickly away, through to that area of strictly guarded privilege where Aubrey could not follow.

Chapter Twelve

They were driving across a sunlit plain bounded in the distance by a line of stony hills. In the car with her were Aubrey, Beatrice and her mother-in-law. It seemed to her they were coming from nowhere in particular and going to nowhere in particular: a meaningless journey in a light-filled void. The hills came nearer. She could see now that there were spindly trees growing on the summit ridges; she could see too how abruptly the stony flanks rose up from the plain. They drove into the shadow thrown by the hills. Looking up, she saw that the upper slopes were honeycombed with black holes.

'Shall we go up and have a look?' Aubrey asked.

They veered off the road, taking a winding track. The plain fell away below them, dissolving into a white, shimmering haze. Higher and higher they climbed, negotiating narrow ledges sliced out of the red rock. She stared at the trees clinging to the ridges and at the black holes pierced in the cliff-face above her.

'What are they?' she asked.

'Tunnels,' Aubrey answered. 'They lead into caves deep inside the hills.'

She did not like being so high up. She did not like being suspended between the blue emptiness of the sky and the shimmering vacuity below her. Her head swam. Desolation enveloped her like a fog. Why was Aubrey bringing her up here? It was so unlike him to go in search of unnecessary adventure. Leaving the car, they moved towards one of those gaping black mouths.

'Why are we here?' she asked. 'Why did you bring me all the way up here?'

'Because I thought it would be interesting to take a look,' Aubrey said. 'I've always wanted to find out what these caves are really like.'

'I don't like it here,' she said. 'Let us go back.'

Beatrice laughed loudly. 'Why?' she asked. 'Why do you want to go back? What are you so afraid of?'

They left the burning day behind them, groping their way through the gloom of the tunnel.

'Why have we come here?' she asked again, her affrighted voice bouncing off the walls. 'I don't like this place. I want light. I want air. I can't breathe properly here. Let us go back.'

'Where do you want to go back to?' her mother-in-law asked. 'How do you know there's anything to go back to? You don't even know where you've come from.'

'All my teaching has been in vain,' Beatrice said.

Inexplicably, Aubrey, Beatrice and her mother-in-law disappeared. Only Beatrice's ribald laughter echoed off the stone. The tunnel broadened. A low dome of rock arched above her head. In the middle of this chamber was a round pool of greyish water.

'Aubrey!' she called out. 'Aubrey! Where are you? I'm afraid, Aubrey. What are we doing here? Why did you bring me here?'

Aubrey did not answer her. No one answered her. Standing on the edge of the stagnant pool, she peered into its filmy depths. Suddenly, without knowing how it happened, she was floundering in that grey water. It closed over her head, its slimy folds sliding over her. She splashed and struggled frantically, vainly seeking solid ground, sinking ever deeper into the cloudy depths. At last she touched bottom. But there was nothing solid upon which she could rest, only a cloying, sucking ooze. With a supreme effort, she managed to free herself from its clutches and rise to the surface. She pulled herself out of the water.

Naked now, she lay as if pinioned to the rock floor of the cave, paralysed in every limb, gasping for air. Aubrey, Beatrice and her mother-in-law had reappeared. Forming a circle, they gazed down upon her with curiosity. Dumbly she stared back at them, unable to restore life to her dead body; unable to find speech and explain herself to them. Beatrice started to laugh. So did her mother-in-law. Aubrey, however, maintained his usual grave demeanour.

'Whatever made you do such a thing?' he asked.

She was exhausted to the point of extinction.

'Whatever made you do such a thing?' Aubrey asked again.

Somehow her voice was restored to her. 'I don't remember how it happened. It just did. Forgive me.'

'What's the good of being sorry when the deed is done?' asked her mother-in-law.

They stood in a circle about her, remote, uncomprehending, withholding all help from her.

Beatrice's laughter resounded through the cave.

Why were they treating her like that? How had she harmed them? She cried out despairingly.

'Dina ... Dina ...' Aubrey's face floated above her.

She stared wildly at the apparition, struggling to restore life to the dead body pinioned to the rock.

Aubrey half-shook, half-massaged her shoulder.

She became quiet, staring up at the floating face.

'You've been having a bad dream,' he said.

Her body was damp; her heart was racing. She closed her eyes. The echoes of Beatrice's laughter continued to resound in her head.

'Just a bad dream,' Aubrey repeated. 'That's all it is. Just a bad dream.' He passed a hand over her moist forehead.

She opened her eyes again, peering warily into the darkness. Through the curtain she could see the blue glow of the electric cross. She heard the steady ticking of the alarm clock. Haltingly, she picked out the shapes of the wardrobe, the dressing table, the chair over which she had flung her clothes.

'You ought to change into something dry,' Aubrey said. He caressed her bony shoulders, her arms. 'You're soaked through. You could catch a chill.'

'Yes,' she replied mechanically. 'I'll change.'

She got out of bed and changed her nightdress. Going to the window, she leaned out into the night, inhaling great gulps of air. High up on the hills the beacon blinked its red warning. She could still hear Beatrice's laughter. Its resonant shrill was caged inside her skull.

*

Dina paused at the familiar cave-like entrance, her face twisting with repugnance. She had always hated coming here. Even more aggravating than that, she hated herself for being there. It was a punishment, a humiliation, she periodically inflicted on herself and it imbued her with a brooding self-disgust. Each visit was a defeat for her and a victory for Madame. After each she vowed never to return. But while she may have given up counting those broken vows, she had not given up making them. Even at that moment, standing there outside the cave-like entrance being jostled by the crowds pushing past her on the narrow pavement, she had not conceded defeat. She could still turn her face away from that darkness, still triumph over the malign impulse that had brought her there.

She remained where she was, relishing and investigating her freedom of will. The two contradictory urges working within her, being in perfect balance, nullified each other and kept her rooted to the spot. The brick tunnel facing her was piled with sacks of charcoal – a charcoal merchant used it as his store-room. It reeked of the open gutter, coated with glaucous slime, running down the middle. It extended murkily for about twenty yards before opening out into a light-filled courtyard forever criss-crossed with lines of dripping washing.

She was in that section of the town dominated by the cavernous halls of the Central Market, by the warehouses of wholesale merchants of many varieties and by ruinous, balconied tenements, built at the turn of the century, harbouring a vagrant population. The surrounding network of streets and lanes was perpetually jammed with lorries, hand-pulled carts and bicycles. There was an abiding miasma of putrefaction hanging over the locality. The blending odours of rank fish, of rotting vegetables and fruit, of blood, of decomposing offal, of stale sweat, fused into a nauseous fog. This miasma not only floated in the air but seemed to ooze out of the asphalt and brick; to infect every surface. One had to walk with care: a permanent slick lubricated the pavements. In the stagnant heat of mid-afternoon, the dirt, the stench, the clamour of horns and bells and voices, became almost unbearable. Madame could, of course, have picked on a more salubrious spot in which to live and carry on her trade. She certainly did not lack the means to do so. All successful practitioners of her art made a lot of money.

For all Dina knew, she might even be reckoned a wealthy woman. But, pleading poverty, she refused to move; adding, with a sly leer, that she was perfectly comfortable where she was. She steadfastly turned down invitations to visit her clients in their homes or elsewhere. Not even the inducement of a handsome bonus could persuade her to do that – though, if rumour was to be believed, she had, once or twice, been seen in the corridors of the Presidential mansion: the occult was known to have a certain appeal for him. It had to be concluded that Madame derived a malicious satisfaction worth more than any amount of money, in dragging her generally sedate clientele to this pestilential quarter of the town.

Hesitating outside the entrance, a fresh surge of detestation and resentment welled up in her. Long ago she had sensed a sort of seething rancour in Madame, verging on hatred. 'You people,' Madame had once observed, 'come here and use me like a public convenience.' After which statement she had laughed. This memory made her wince. Over the couple of years or so since she had been first brought into contact with the 'witch' (as Beatrice, who had effected the introduction, called her), she must have expended several hundred dollars. Fortunately, Aubrey was not the kind of man to enquire into the outlets of her expenditure. She could do exactly as she pleased with what he gave her every month and no questions were ever asked. Not once had he called her to account. Perhaps he should have done. But that was not his way. Kind, trusting, considerate Aubrey! What would he say if he could see her now lurking outside this tunnel? There arose before her those big, dark, compassionate eyes. Again Dina winced.

Aubrey himself was no stranger to the occult. An entire corner of the bookshop was devoted to works of a mystical tendency. The knowledge he had gained from them formed a conspicuous element of his polymathic capacity. He talked familiarly of Paracelsus and occasionally would deploy terms such as metempsychosis. He had, as well, a pack of Tarot cards: its symbolisms, he explained, intrigued him. Once, in a playful way, he had offered to read her fortune from the Tarot. The thought of Aubrey – even in jest – interpreting her fate had appalled her. She had rejected the suggestion, feigning complete indifference. Yet, despite all this, his involvement in such matters was largely literary. It would never have occurred to him to consult a self-appointed mercenary like Madame.

Her visits to Madame were rooted in quite another soil. It was not a fascination with the occult as such which led her to that tunnel; it was not a simple desire to know what was going to happen to her in the next month or two that brought her there – just as it is not always a simple desire for physical gratification that brings a man to a harlot's door. She came because it was only here, in the presence of this sneering, hostile woman, into whose waiting palms she emptied her purse ... it was only here that she was able, after a fashion, to expose and acknowledge herself to herself: a voluptuous self-surrender. Her need to do so was not entirely dissimilar in its imperative nature from the overpowering urge to sexual fulfilment. How could she have begun to explain this impulsion to Aubrey? It was not possible for her to reveal an appetite so elemental and so squalid. Even Beatrice would not have understood: her daring, often more apparent than real, never overstepped certain limits; her instinct of self-preservation ran true and ran deep. It was precisely this instinct that wavered in Dina, fomenting a black exhilaration, a black yearning. It might have been no good to her if Madame had consented to leave her lair and see her in a place of her own choosing. Maybe she needed to make this journey to this quarter of the town, to inhale its suppurating odours. Lurking outside the entrance to the tunnel, she was revolted by her condition. Her skin prickled and itched in the mid-afternoon heat.

More than two months had passed since she had last stood there. It was the longest interval she had managed to sustain between visits. To that extent, she could congratulate herself. On leaving the house she had not conceded it was here she intended to come. Just as, even while standing outside the entrance, she had not conceded that she was necessarily going to walk in there and climb the stairs to the top of the tenement. She stood there, debating with herself, testing her freedom and power of will.

From a little blue-painted bar on the opposite side of the narrow street poured the pounding rhythms of a juke-box. Its exterior was adorned with crude but colourful renderings of jiving blacks. However, the centrepiece, occupying almost a whole wall, portrayed an imagined African landscape. It showed an extensive grassland, bordered by hills, watered by many rivers, dotted with lions, zebras, giraffes and hippopotamuses. Flocks of white birds populated the blue sky. These decorations were a recent refinement. They

171

had not been there on her previous visit to Madame. Within the bar she saw a large framed photograph of the President. Above it was affixed a printed exhortation.

One People! One Party! One Redeemer!

She became aware that she was being scrutinised. A young man, bearded, hair plaited, a knitted cap clamped like a bowl on his head, was staring at her from the doorway of the bar. She realised, with sudden alarm, how conspicuous she must be, loitering there in her sleeveless, salmon-coloured dress, wearing dark glasses that hid nearly half of her face, a tasselled leather handbag hanging over one shoulder, her open-work shoes displaying shining, red-painted toenails. She looked away from the hostile face in the doorway. A man carrying a bulky load on his back bumped into her. The rancid odour of his sweat enveloped her. She swayed away from him, in the process almost losing her balance on the slippery pavement.

'Is something you looking for, Miss? Or somebody?'

Startled, she glanced down at the questioner, a wrinkled crone crouched a few feet away from her, selling little heaps of sun-baked fruit arranged on a tray. The creature regarded her dispassionately.

Abruptly, as if propelled by some outside force, she set off down the tunnel, making her way between the sacks of charcoal. She came to the wooden stairs. Again she hesitated. A woman, pegging out lines of dripping washing in the courtyard, paused to look at her. Some naked children, laughing and shouting, were splashing themselves at a standpipe. She started the ascent, her eyes fixed straight ahead of her. The stairway was poorly lit and encrusted with dirt. A faint smell of urine mingled with the stagnant odours of stale cooking. On the landings, doors leading into lightless warrens were thrown wide open. From within, old women and children stared at her. She climbed swiftly to the top of the building.

She reached the familiar, green-painted door with its brass

knocker shaped like a lion's paw. She stopped to catch her breath. Daylight seeped through a cracked window coated with grime. She looked down into the courtyard at the criss-crossing lines of washing. The children at the stand-pipe were still laughing and shouting, their bodies glistening in the sunlight. She lifted the lion's paw. Inside, she could hear coughing, groans, reluctant stirrings – the unmistakable sounds of Miss Bertha. The door opened a crack, no more than its security chains would allow. Miss Bertha's rheumy eyes stared at her. A flannel cloth was wrapped around her head. She exuded medicinal vapours, compounded in the main of bay-rum and camphor. Miss Bertha's collapsed, toothless mouth worked ceaselessly, futilely, as she scanned the visitor.

Images of murderous assault nearly always presented themselves when she came here. She would think of Dos-toievski's Raskolnikov armed with his axe. How easy it would be to come in here one day with a machete and slaughter these two old women whose lives could hardly have mattered to anyone except themselves. She would imagine herself carrying out the deed – suddenly revealing the machete, raising it with a cry of triumph, bringing it down on their soft skulls; she imagined the expressions of helpless terror and disbelief that would contort their faces. Indeed, it was a cause for surprise that they had survived all these years without coming to any harm in their little eyrie. Madame must have an indecent fortune stacked under her mattress. She was an ideal candidate for Raskolnikovian attack. But this, alas, was not St Petersburg. Madame might very well be murdered one of these days, but there would be no Raskol-nikovs involved. Her death, whether violent or peaceful, would have no redeeming qualities; no metaphysical gla-mour: it would be without meaning.

Miss Bertha, mouth ceaselessly working, scanned her face. At length, recognition dawned. After a spasm of fumb-ling, she managed to unhook both the chains that secured the door, making a space just wide enough to permit entry. Miss Bertha glanced suspiciously down the gloomy stairway before closing the door. After another spasm of fumbling, she succeeded in replacing the chains. The room was flooded with dusty sunshine. A strip of red carpet, mottled with threadbare patches, covered the floor. To the left was a wooden partition rising to the ceiling. Behind that was the cubby-hole of a 'studio' where Madame received her clients. Her insinuating buzz penetrated the partition. To the right was a curtained alcove.

The room was crowded with furniture and bric-à-brac. A sofa of cracked leather and two matching armchairs were arranged around a low, carved table; there was a grandfather clock with only an hour hand; there were chests of drawers; there were footstools upholstered in faded velvet; there was a Bible lying open on a reading stand. Paintings of flowers and ships decorated the walls. Ornaments of brass and glass and porcelain were haphazardly arranged on sagging shelves. Vases ornamented with Chinese dragons stood on the floor. Some of these were filled with bouquets of paper flowers, their petals and stems coated with dust.

'The old witch probably doesn't even suspect the value of some of the stuff she has in there,' Beatrice had said. She had made offers to buy certain items. Madame, typically, had refused to sell. This had enraged Beatrice. She accused her of ingratitude. 'If it wasn't for me,' she said, 'the old witch wouldn't be where she is now. I've brought her way some real VIPs – let me assure you of that. Some *real* VIPs.' 'Maybe you should arrange to have her murdered one day,' Dina had replied, amused by her rancour. Beatrice laughed. 'Don't tempt me. She deserves to die a horrible death. What's going to happen to all that stuff when she finally kicks the bucket?' 'Perhaps,' Dina said, 'she plans to take it all with her. To have buried beside her all her treasure, as certain ancient kings used to do. She might even take Miss Bertha along with her.'

Catching a spectral glimpse of herself in a gilt-framed mirror, Dina quickly looked away. Miss Bertha, exhaling camphor and bay-rum, spoke behind her.

'Is Sister expecting you?' she asked.

'No ...' She listened to the murmur coming from behind the partition.

'You didn't make an appointment?'

'No ... I didn't make an appointment. If she's too busy to see me, I'll go.' She made a half-hearted move towards the door.

Miss Bertha stayed her. She shuffled across to the partition and knocked gingerly. Madame growled in response. Miss Bertha opened the door and poked her head within. Closing the door, she shuffled back towards the sofa.

'Sister will see you,' she whispered. 'But you going to have to wait.'

She was torn. Even now she could escape. But she let herself be led by Miss Bertha across to the curtained alcove. Miss Bertha pushed her in and drew the curtain. This alcove was one of Madame's few concessions to the sensibilities of her clients – who, on the whole, did not much like running into each other. If, for instance, they encountered each other on the stairs, faces would be averted as they sidled past. Madame and Miss Bertha did what was in their power to isolate their visitors. Accidents, though, did happen.

The alcove was furnished in the style of a down-at-heel doctor's or dentist's waiting room. Two or three chairs were grouped about a round, glass-topped table piled with out-of-date English and American magazines. Too often had she lurked in there, invisible behind its floral curtain, waiting to be summoned to Madame's presence. Now she went across to the window. The children had finished their bathing and disappeared from the courtyard. So had the washerwoman. She looked out across the jumble of rooftops, through the brassy glare of the afternoon, at the grey harbour which rippled with an oily, viscous swell.

She had spent all her life in this town. Looking out at its derelict perspectives, it seemed to her that she was looking out at no more than an extension of herself. She and the city were one. When she ventured into it, it was like venturing into an inalienable part of herself. What she saw, what she heard, what she felt, held no revelations for her. All its perspectives were well-trodden pathways through her brain. She knew its rank odours when, after a heavy shower of rain, the glistening streets steamed under the raw blast of the sun breaking through the clouds. She knew the days – like today – when the humid air trembled and shimmered and the sky was white and dead at three o'clock in the afternoon. She knew its brief, purple dusks and its thick, starry darknesses. She felt she knew the shape of every leaf, the texture of every stone, the rustle of every warm breeze. Each had impressed on her a fossilised trace. She knew the faces and voices of the government clerks, the shop girls, the beggars, all of whom, at bottom, seemed to have one face and speak with one voice.

It was summed up for her by those Sunday afternoons when you lay in a darkened bedroom with nothing to do, drowned in the afternoon silence, mesmerised by the slow rotations of the ceiling fan, the mind ballooning with vacancy, stunned by its own emptiness. There came to her an almost forgotten image of herself sprawled on a bed, watching with torpid fascination a mosquito that had settled on her wrist. She had watched it feed on her, letting it grow bloated with her blood; until, sated, it had floated lethargically away and come to rest on the wall behind her.

The vacancy . . . you could not get away from it for long. Whichever way you turned, there it was, lying in wait for you. She thought of the time when she had yearned to sail in a big, white ship out of that harbour upon whose oily swell she now gazed, to escape forever the sun-stunned vacuum and live another kind of life somewhere else. But, gradually, recognising the impossibility of escape, the yearning had died. Somehow, it had oozed away until she could say, not without truth, that she no longer cared what happened to her. Yet, to say it had oozed away was not quite correct. It would be more accurate to say that she had let it go ... let go of it ... and allowed the vision of redemption – those fleeting intimations of richness, of possibility, which sometimes welled up in her – to recede from her and eventually die.

Miss Bertha had drifted off to sleep again and was snoring. Now and again she emitted startled grunts and seemed to be on the verge of choking to death. At other times she would break into an incoherent babble. Then she would fall quiet and the cycle would start all over again. She picked up one of the magazines piled on the glass table. The pages were tacky and fraying at the edges. She paused at an advertisement which showed a group of elegantly dressed men and women sitting at a candle-lit table. To judge from the picturesque disorder of knives and forks, crumpled napkins, scattered crumbs, bits of cheese and half-empty bottles of wine, they had just finished eating. A bowl-shaped lampshade hung low over the centre of the table. Cigarette smoke coiled up towards it. There was laughter on every face. Someone had evidently made a witty remark. Beyond the table was a marble fireplace heaped with glowing coals. Above it hung a mirror reproducing the happy scene.

Next door Miss Bertha wheezed and coughed and babbled.

She idly turned the pages, pausing at another of the advertisements. This one showed a man on a white horse riding through a misty, sylvan landscape. A half-clad woman, freshly risen out of the foam of her luxurious ablutions, watched him dreamily from a window.

Next door Miss Bertha wheezed and coughed and dreamed of demons.

Putting aside the magazine, she listened to Madame's honeyed murmurings leaking through the partition. She was

177

herself close to dozing off, beginning to dream of her own demons, when she was suddenly roused by the irruption of Madame and her client into the sitting room.

'If you do as I tell you,' Madame was saying, 'everything will turn out to your advantage. Have no fear.'

The man mumbled self-effacingly. No doubt he was aware of her presence behind the curtain. She suspected Madame of relishing these situations.

'Come back and see me in a month's time.' Madame spoke like a doctor now. 'Let me know how you've progressed.'

The man promised that he would; the door opened and closed. His footfalls faded rapidly down the stairs. Madame returned to her studio. She was not called immediately because Madame liked to rest a little between her consultations. She experienced the tingle of anticipation that nearly always accompanied these moments. The effect produced was like that induced by a quick intake of alcohol. She surrendered to the illicit warmth of the sensation. After a few minutes Miss Bertha parted the screen and announced that Sister was ready to receive her.

Madame was sitting at a table placed in the centre of the room. Her head was thrown back and her eyes were closed. Her stubby fingers were splayed out on the edge of the table. Without opening her eyes Madame indicated by a languid, downward sweep of her plump arm that she should take a seat opposite her. Miss Bertha drew out the chair. She sat down. Miss Bertha retreated, glancing with nervous deference at her sister as she did so.

The studio was dark and airless. Madame did not stir. The noises of the city were muted by the closed windows. Along one wall was a narrow bed where Madame, when she was especially exhausted, was sometimes to be found lying with a damp towel covering her face. On the other side of the room was a glass-doored cabinet in which she stored the tools of her trade – manuals on palmistry, astrological charts, a

178

crystal ball. Dina had never seen her make use of any of these things. To divert herself, she studied Madame's double chin, her thick, short neck, the smooth mounds of her cheeks which shone as if they had been dipped in oil, the flattened, gaping triangles of her nostrils.

Presently, Madame opened her eyes and lowered her head. She blinked rapidly several times.

'Well, my dear,' she murmured, her shining cheeks swelling into their usual leer, 'how can I help you? Tell me.'

*

Dina breathed in deeply when she stepped out from the premature twilight that had invaded the tenement and emerged into the crowded street. A film of gluey sweat polished her cheeks and forehead. She walked swiftly, making her way through the network of congested lanes leading away from the market. The asphalt wafted up acrid fumes; the smells of food being prepared in a hundred cramped rooms swirled out of open windows and doorways. It was as if the city, having held its breath during the dead hours of the day, was engaged in a slow, protracted exhalation. As ever, she railed at herself for wasting her time, wasting her money; for defiling herself to no purpose at all.

Throughout Madame had sat in feline repose, plump fingers resting on the edge of the table, saying little. Occasionally, she stretched and yawned, not taking the trouble to cover her mouth. Her eyes, registering no emotion, stared out at her from between their folds of flesh. Next door Miss Bertha had snored and broken out into garbled incantation.

'You keep on saying you 'fraid,' Madame had interrupted. 'But 'fraid of what? What it have for you to be 'fraid of?'

'I don't know,' Dina said.

Madame had started to laugh. Dina jumped up from her chair. She flung her fee on the table and watched how calmly those plump fingers had encircled the notes. She had fled into the sitting-room, jolting Miss Bertha out of her slum-

179

bers and, before the old woman had had a chance to move or even realise what was happening, she had unhooked the security chains and raced down the stairs. It was only when she had regained the tunnel that she realised her vision was blurred by tears. There, among the stacks of charcoal, she had dried her eyes and collected herself. Even now as she walked along, her vision would blur and the muscles in her chest would tighten until they ached.

She came to the square fenced in with rust-red iron railings, formerly named after Queen Victoria, now called after the National Hero, Boniface. The statue of the Queen had been pulled down, replaced by a piece of muscular sculpture which depicted Boniface snapping his fetters with one hand and, in the other, holding aloft a gun. She strolled towards the fountain. The spray had been turned off – a municipal gesture of thrift in a time of water shortage. All kinds of debris – rotting leaves, cigarette packs, bits of newspaper, tin cans – were embedded in the mossy ooze collected in the base of the bowl. People sprawled in the speckled shade of the tamarind trees. Tired out by her walk, she sat down on a ruinous bench. Not far away a tall Negro, dressed in a white robe, his hair plaited into ropy strands, a silver cross dangling from his neck, preached hoarsely. As he spoke, he boxed the air with his fists and waved a Bible above his head.

'Jehovah going to come with a sword of fire to smite the iniquitous. He going to punish those who been punishing us. Have no fear. The day of deliverance is at hand. The tongues of the oppressors going to be torn out of their mouths. Their eyeballs going to rot in their sockets. Their flesh going to fall from their bones. That day coming. It almost here. We going to be free at last. Is written.' His arms punched the air; the sweat flowed in streams down his face.

'Hail Jehovah!' chorused a group of women also dressed in white. 'Hail our Redeemer! Hail our Liberator!' They clapped their hands, chanted and danced about the preacher. Several of them carried portraits of the President.

180

Others banged tambourines. She stared at the preacher, who was reading from the Bible now, his voice rough with emotion and effort, his face glistening. She rose from the bench, walking slowly, going past the statue of Boniface, crossing the square to the street on the far side. Soon the angry declamation faded behind her, drowned by the roar of the traffic.

She went on homeward, her shadow stretched out behind her. The pavement was lined with stalls tended by young men adorned with locks of tangled hair. A pulsing fog of primal rhythm vibrated through the yellow afternoon. The humid air was scented with the sweet and portentous fumes of marijuana. Slowly, the city seemed to be sinking into some more elemental realm of being, becoming blurred with unnamed threats and mysteries; shot through with a novel and delirious barbarism. She passed a block of burnt-out buildings, an acre or more of twisted metal and charred beams, fenced in with corrugated iron which was daubed with Plebiscite slogans and peeling photographs of the President. On that site had stood a department store, cool and spacious and dark, smelling of leather, of bolts of cloth. At Christmas, the interior would be festooned with coloured lanterns, big bells made of crêpe paper, bellying strands of tinsel.

A cooler current of air fanned and freshened her cheeks. The broad sweep of Independence Park opened out in front of her. She crossed the road. A small wind, irradiated with the day's staleness and dying heat, was blowing in irregular gusts, churning up the dust, fomenting miniature whirlwinds. The loungers were out in force, perched like vultures on the sagging rails that fenced in the park. A haze of litter – banana skins, orange peel, peanut shells, coconut husks, tin cans, bottles, plastic bags – fogged the grassy verge bordering the path. Many of the green-painted wooden benches were no more than rotting stumps embedded in their crumbling concrete platforms. The asphalt path itself was buckling and cracked and pockmarked with holes.

Say Yes To The People And No To The Exploiters.

The slogan, daubed in streaks of red, was repeated at intervals on the asphalt.

Nothing was ever repaired or even replaced. Whatever began to crumble was allowed to go on crumbling. Decay was the only recognisable law in this place. It was as if those who lived here did not merely have no use for beauty and order but were hostile to their very existence.

She paused opposite the Park Hotel. She stared up at its tiers of moss-stained balconies, each crowned by an intricate arabesque of wrought-iron fretwork. It was odd now to recall the awe it used to inspire in her. Not until she was grown up had she penetrated its portals. In fact, it was only in the years immediately preceding Independence that people like herself had been freely permitted to enjoy its refinements. As a child, on their Sunday family walks around the park, she would gaze into its sombrely lit, carpeted lobby enclosed by panelled walls. Beyond, she would catch a glimpse of the inner sanctum of the dining room. The tables there were spread with white cloths and over each one hung a wicker-shaded lamp.

The hotel was a muted, mysterious temple, subsisting in a state of abstraction from its surroundings. What rites were enacted within was anybody's guess. It was never said that they couldn't enter there. At least, she never recalled anything being said. It was as if knowledge of the taboo suffused the air surrounding the place, making questions and explanations quite unnecessary. The Park Hotel had simply been part of an enigmatic order which had nothing to do with her or with anyone remotely like her. Beyond that, her childish probing did not penetrate. How strange it was in later years to hear others talk of the 'Colour Bar'. How strange and how dispiriting it was to discover what the 'Colour Bar' was: to discover that behind the enigma lay a truth so stark, so tawdry, so unredeeming. It was like pushing aside a richly veined rock to reveal, on its lichenous underside, a suppurating colony of maggots. A secret which

182

had been kept hidden for so long had been dragged out into the open. A conspiracy of silence had been broken. She almost regretted that it had had to happen.

But the discovery was part of their new knowledge of the world and it was not to be avoided. Demonstrations had occurred. The mob had paraded with placards and banners in front of the hotel. Stones and bottles had been hurled. One or two windows had been smashed. On the streets whites had been harassed and manhandled. The Colour Bar ... discovery of its existence had overnight made everything that had ever transpired within that hallowed gloom sickening and unforgivable. It had suddenly begun to hurt. She had acquired a retrospective disgust for her innocence, her acquiescence, on those prim Sunday circumambulations of the park. Her father must have known. Why had he never said anything? Why had he never taken offence? How, Sunday after Sunday, dressed up to the nines, could they have walked past that insult to their existence and remain unmoved? She felt that she had been betrayed on those Sunday walks.

'You must have known you could never set foot in there,' she said to her father one day. 'How did that make you feel?'

'It didn't make me feel anything,' he replied evenly, 'because I never thought about it.'

'But why did you never think about it, Papa?'

'Why?' He had gazed at her blankly – as if the question eluded his comprehension. 'Because it was none of my business,' he answered finally. 'Because I had other things to worry about. If the white people wanted to be by themselves, how did that harm me? Let them be by themselves! I wasn't going to run after anybody begging to be admitted to the human race.'

He refused to talk any more about it. That remark of his – about not begging to be admitted to the human race – had startled her at the time. It was more than a rebuke: it had affected her like a slap in the face. At the time, though, its only effect had been to aggravate her anger at him; to augment her contempt. Only now could she guess at the cornered pride that must have prompted it; at the pain and defiance it simultaneously concealed and expressed. She felt a new respect, a new pity, for him. Thinking of his fate, a fresh wound was opened up in her. It was far too late to say she was sorry.

He had spoken truly. Their hurt and rage was the hurt and rage of the despised and rejected; the hurt and rage of those who had suddenly found out that they had been left outside and were naked, defenceless and redundant. It was shocking news. They banged furiously on every door that was shut against them, seeking to be let in. They had been fooled and cheated. But fooled and cheated out of what? Out of the knowledge of their condition. That, in the end, was the true oppression. They had been duped.

Rubbing the sleep out of their eyes, they had gazed in astonishment at the world and they had wanted a new world of their own making. That was the answer most of them had been schooled to give – and still gave when pressed. A new, uncontaminated world of their own making. On the surface, the talk was of freedom, justice, equality and brotherhood. That was what Aubrey would have said he wanted. That was what she, for a while, would have said she wanted.

But, down deep in their hearts, the mob did not want to create. Creation was not possible for them. Or for Aubrey. Or for herself. They had not the faintest notion of how to set about the task – or, even, what it was they would really like to create. The words they mouthed, the slogans with which they adorned their banners and their placards, were mere froth churned by the chaos. When they paused and looked into themselves – what did they find? Nothing!

A void. Darkness. Unspecified hunger. That was all they had – their emptiness, their darkness, their hunger. They did not have a self, a soul, to call their own. That was what they had been cheated out of: selves, souls. It was a terrible discovery which they sought to disguise by their displays of frenzy, by their wild dreams of a return to Africa, by their ecstatic and compulsive sloganeering. Before this delirium, freedom, justice, equality and brotherhood melted away into spectral absurdity. The only genuine desire left was the desire to destroy.

To wreak vengeance. To tear down. To burn. To loot. To insult. To kill. The President and the men who surrounded him understood perfectly. They were not led astray by spectres: they were realists. And, most important of all, the void and hunger were within them too. Cheated out of a self, the mob would not be cheated out of its anguish.

It was almost dark when she turned the corner. She paused near the spot where she had seen the card. However, she did not look down into the gutter but stared at the defaced wall of the church.

Kill The Nigger In You.

One Nation. One Party. One Redeemer.

The echo of a faint detonation rippled through the twilight.

'I will lift up mine eyes unto the hills . . .'

Her attention was caught by the boom of a distant loudspeaker, breaking the stillness, spewing exhortation into the night. Borne on the wind, the source of the disturbance seemed to come closer. She strained to hear what was being said, to extract meaning from the dim, oceanic roar. But only its frenzy, its orgiastic rage, communicated itself. Gradually, it ebbed away, swallowed back into the stillness.

She walked slowly towards the fluorescent glow of the bookshop.